This book belongs to:

..........................................

This edition © The Bodley Head Children's Books 2000
Freelance editor: Sally Byford

1 3 5 7 9 10 8 6 4 2

First published in Great Britain 2000
by The Bodley Head Children's Books
Random House, 20 Vauxhall Bridge Road, London SW1V 2SA

Random House Australia (Pty) Limited
20 Alfred Street, Milsons Point, Sydney
New South Wales 2061, Australia

Random House New Zealand Limited
18 Poland Road, Glenfield
Auckland 10, New Zealand

Random House South Africa (Pty) Limited
Endulini, 5A Jubilee Road,
Parktown 2193, South Africa

THE RANDOM HOUSE GROUP Limited Reg. No 954009
www.randomhouse.co.uk

A CIP catalogue record for this book is available from the British Library

ISBN 0 370 32682 2

Printed and bound in Singapore by Tien Wah Press (PTE) Ltd

# THE Shirley Hughes COLLECTION

THE BODLEY HEAD
LONDON

# Contents

## PART TWO, Stories and Poems for Young Children

**PART THREE,** Stories and Poems for Older Children

PART FOUR, Stories for all to enjoy

*To my family*

# Introduction

Seeing this collection come together, right from the first conception, has been an exhilarating experience for me. Now here it is: handsomely produced and encompassing so much of the work I have done over the years, from the simplest picture stories which address my very youngest audience - just out of the board book stage and raring to go - to a hitherto unpublished story written for BBC Radio Four. The seamless dovetailing of this wide range of material into one volume has been achieved by the superb expertise of the editorial and design team at Random House. They have ensured that each story, though redesigned, is delivered intact and its flavour retained. There have been urgent telephone calls and weighty deliberations, not so much about what we should put in but what we could bear to leave out.

I can hardly believe they are all here; all my familiar characters, as well as stories I have written for slightly older children and ones I have illustrated for other authors in both colour and line. My other publishers, Walker Books, Penguin and Egmont among others, have lent themselves to the project with great generosity, allowing this collection to be a truly comprehensive one. It's great to see my exuberant small heroine from *The Nursery Collection* here with her baby brother; and Lucy and Tom who, had they marched with real time, would now be in their early forties and no doubt raising families of their own. And, of course, Alfie, who made his first appearance with his little sister Annie Rose in 1981 is still celebrating with other four and five year olds at his friend Bernard's birthday party. Like all fictional children they remain perennially the same age. Only Dogger has grown old in the real world and now lives in tranquil retirement in my workroom. He doesn't go about much. The Book Tour life style no longer suits him, but he is still gamely providing me with encouragement and inspiration.

It is, of course, my readers who keep these fictional characters alive. It is profoundly satisfying, and humbling too, for me to be enabled to introduce them in this splendid form to yet another up-and-coming audience.

# PART ONE

Stories and Rhymes for the
Nursery Years

# Fingers

One little finger
Dancing on her own,
Joined by another one,
Now she's not alone.
Up jumps the middle one,
Strong and tall,

Here comes the fourth one,
Liveliest of all.
Stubby old Tom Thumb
Has nowhere to go,
Put him with the others
And there's five in a row.

# Toes

Beatie Bo,
Big toe.
Mrs Moore,
Next door.
Solomon Riddle,
In the middle.
Lucky Jim,
Next to him.

And last of all,
Curled up small,
Fat little Billy Ball.

# Bathwater's Hot

Bathwater's hot,

Seawater's cold;

Ginger's kittens are very young,

But Buster's getting old.

Some things you can throw away,

Some are nice to keep;

Here's someone who is wide awake...

Shhh, he's fast asleep!

Some things are hard as stone,
Some are soft as cloud;

Whisper very quietly,

Shout OUT LOUD!

It's fun to run
very fast,

Or to be slow;

The red light
says "stop",

And the green
light says "go".

It's kind to be helpful,

Unkind to tease;

Rather rude to push and grab,
Polite to say "please".

Night-time is dark,

Daytime is light;

The sun says
"good morning",

Good night !

And the moon
says "good night".

# Bernard

I like Bernard.

Rough Bernard,

Tough Bernard,

Stop-it-that's-quite-enough Bernard,

Playing pirates, running races,

Wrinkled socks and trailing laces,

Funny jokes and wild faces,

Falling-about Bernard,

Scuffle-and-shout Bernard,

I like Bernard.

# Girl Friends

Marian, Lily and Annie Rose
Are three bonny girls, as everyone knows.
Sometimes bouncy, sometimes sad,
Sometimes sleepy, sometimes glad,
Sometimes grubby, sometimes clean,
Often kind, though sometimes mean.
But most of the time they try to be good,
And to all that know them it's understood
That Marian, Lily and Annie Rose
Are best of friends, as everyone knows.

# Mudlarks

I like mud.
The slippy, sloppy, squelchy kind,

The slap-it-into-pies kind.

Stir it up in puddles,
Slither and slide.

I *do* like mud.

# Wind

I like the wind.

The soft, summery, gentle kind,

The gusty, blustery, fierce kind.

Ballooning out the curtains,

Blowing things about,

Wild and wilful everywhere.

I *do* like the wind.

# Lucy and Tom at the Seaside

One hot day Lucy and Tom and their mum and dad
thought they would go to the seaside.

Lucy is helping to pack up the picnic. There are
sandwiches and hard-boiled eggs, apples, biscuits and a bottle
of orange squash. There is also a lovely chocolate cake.

Tom goes off to find the buckets and spades in the sandpit.

They go to the seaside in the train.

Tom keeps asking when they are going to get to the sea.

Lucy wears her armbands in the train so as to be all ready to swim when they get there.

At last they've arrived! They walk down a rather long road carrying all the picnic things and bathing bags and buckets and spades.

There's a very special seasidey smell.

And there's the sea!

It's much bigger than either Lucy or Tom had ever remembered.

They run straight down to where the waves are coming up
on to the wet sand and walk along the edge.

There are a lot of other children on the beach, as well
as mothers and fathers and babies and grannies and people
paddling, and dogs who dash in and out of the water,
barking excitedly at seagulls.

Lucy and Tom want to swim right away, so they all put on their bathing suits and go into the sea, hand in hand. Lucy and Dad do some swimming.

The sea is much rougher
and splashier than the
swimming pool near home.

It's harder to swim in,
but much more fun.

Tom likes being chased
by the waves.

After the swim Mum helps everyone to rub dry and they
play a running-about game to get warm.

They settle down to their picnic.

Several wasps try to join in.

The tide is coming in.

Dad helps Lucy and Tom to make a beautiful sand castle. It has turrets covered in shells and stones, a moat, and a tunnel going right through the middle and coming out the other side.

Slowly the moat fills up with water, then the tunnel.

Soon only the top turret is left.

Then nothing at all.

A lot of interesting things are happening on the beach.

There are people flying kites and playing cricket and ball games.

Two little girls are burying their father's legs in the sand so that only his toes are sticking out.

Some people are trying to get in or out of their bathing suits under towels, which is very difficult.

Lucy and Tom play in a rock-pool.

Lucy finds lots of different kinds of seaweed and some shells which she puts into her bucket.

Tom finds some stones and a crab's claw.

Lucy makes a face in the sand. It has stones for eyes, a row of little shells for teeth, and a lot of seaweedy hair.

Mum helps Tom make a speedboat pointing right out to sea.

Further up the beach there are some donkeys. Lucy and Tom ask if they can have a ride.

Lucy's donkey is grey with white legs. His name – "Pepsi" – is written on his harness.

Tom's donkey is brown and is called "Cola".

It's nearly time to go home. Mum is packing up the picnic things. There's just time for a last ice-cream.

Lucy writes her name in very big letters in the wet sand.

Then she writes Tom's name too.

It's been a *lovely* day.

# A Picture of Annie Rose

Two brown eyes,
One pink nose,
Ten busy fingers,
Ten pink toes.

Colour in her brown curls,
Colour in her clothes,
Colour in a big smile
And that's Annie Rose.

# Wet

Dark clouds,
Rain again,
Rivers on the
Misted pane.
Wet umbrellas
In the street,
Running noses,
Damp feet.

# Misty

Mist in the morning,
Raw and nippy,
Leaves on the pavement,
Wet and slippy.
Sun on fire
Behind the trees,
Muddy boots,
Muddy knees.

Shop windows,
Lighted early,
Soaking grass,
Dewy, pearly.
Red, lemon,
Orange and brown,
Silently, softly,
The leaves float down.

# Cold

Cold fingers,
Cold toes,
Pink sky,
Pink nose.
Hard ground,
Bare trees,
Branches crack,
Puddles freeze.
Frost white,
Sun red,
Warm room,
Warm bed.

# PART TWO

Stories and Poems for
Young Children

# Fallen Giant

A big tree
lying down
is like a giant
with torn-out roots
instead of feet.
It's like a ship
sailing far out to sea,
or a house with many rooms.
It has places to hide
and swing on
and climb along.
A big tree
lying down
is a good place to play.
But you can never make it stand up again.
Not ever.

# Dogger

Once there was a soft brown toy called Dogger. One of his ears pointed upwards and the other flopped over. His fur was worn in places because he was quite old. He belonged to Dave.

Dave was *very* fond of Dogger.
He took him everywhere.

Sometimes he gave him
rides in a trolley.

Sometimes he pulled him
along on a lead made of
string like a real dog.

When it was cold
he wrapped him up
in a bit of blanket.

Now and again Dave's Mum said that Dogger was
getting much too dirty. She showed Dave how to
wash him in a bowl of soapy water. Then they
hung him up by his tail on the washing-line to dry.

Dave's baby brother, Joe, liked hard toys. He liked putting
them in his mouth and biting on them, because he was getting teeth.
Dave's big sister, Bella, took seven teddies to bed with her every night.
She had to sleep right up against the wall to stop herself from falling out.
But Dave liked only Dogger.

One afternoon Dave and Mum set out to collect Bella from school. Mum took Joe in the pushchair and Dave took Dogger. Next to the school gate where the mums waited was a playing-field. Some men with ladders were putting up coloured flags. Mum said that there was going to be a Summer Fair to get money to buy things for the school. Dave pushed Dogger up against the railings to show him what was going on.

Just then the children started to come out of school.

An ice-cream van came round the corner playing a tune. Bella ran up with her satchel flying.

"Mum, can we have an ice-cream?"

Mum gave her the money for two cones. Joe didn't have a whole ice-cream to himself because he was too dribbly.

On the way home
Dave walked beside the pushchair
giving Joe licks off his ice-cream. Joe kicked
his feet about and shouted for more in-between licks.

    At tea-time Dave was rather quiet.

    In the bath he was even quieter.

    At bed-time he said:

"I want Dogger."

But Dogger was nowhere to be found.

Mum looked under the bed.

She looked behind
the cupboard.

She searched in the kitchen –

– and underneath the stairs.
Dave watched anxiously through
the banisters. Joe watched through
the bars of his cot.

Bella joined in to look for Dogger. She turned out her own
toy-box in case he was in there, but he wasn't.

When Dad came home he looked for Dogger too. He
searched in the shed and down the garden path with a torch.

But Dogger was quite lost.

Dave was very sad when he went to bed.
Bella kindly lent him one of her teddies to go to sleep with
but it was not the same thing as Dogger. Dave kept waking
up in the night and missing him.

The next day was Saturday
and they all went to the School
Summer Fair. The playing-field
was full of stalls and side-shows.

There was a Fancy Dress Parade.

Then there were Sports, with an Egg-and-Spoon Race –

a Wheelbarrow Race

and a Fathers' Race.

Bella was very good at races.
She won the Three-Legged
Race with her friend Barbara.

"Wouldn't you like to go in
for a race?" they asked Dave.
But Dave didn't feel like racing.
He was missing Dogger too much.

Then another very exciting
thing happened to Bella.
She won first
prize in a
Raffle!

It was a huge yellow Teddy Bear, wearing a beautiful
blue silk bow. He was almost as big as Dave.

Dave didn't like that Teddy at all. At that moment
he didn't like Bella much either because she kept on
winning things. He went off on his own to look at
the stalls.

One lady had a Toy Stall, full of knitted ducks and cars
and baby dolls in bonnets. And there, at the very back
of the stall, behind a lot of other toys, was —

# DOGGER!

He was wearing a ticket saying "5p".

There were a lot of people round the stall. Dave tried to explain to the lady that it was his Dogger, who had got lost and somehow been put on the stall by mistake, but she wasn't listening. He looked in his pocket. He had 3p but that wasn't enough. He ran to find Mum and Dad to ask them to buy Dogger back *at once*.

Dave went everywhere in the crowd but he couldn't see Mum and Dad. He thought he was going to cry. At last he found Bella by the cakes. When she heard about Dogger, she and Dave ran back to the Toy Stall as fast as they could.

But something terrible had happened. Dogger had just been bought by a little girl!

She was already walking off with him. Dave began to cry.

Bella ran after her and tried to explain that Dogger really belonged to Dave, and could they please buy him back?

But the little girl said: "No."

She said that she had bought Dogger with her own money and she wanted him. She held on to him very tightly.

Dave cried and cried.

And the little girl started to cry too.

But out of the corner of her eye she caught sight of Bella's big yellow Teddy. She stopped crying and put out her hand to stroke his beautiful blue silk bow.

Then Bella did something *very* kind.

"Would you swop this Teddy for my brother's dog, then?" she asked.
Right away the little girl stopped crying and began to smile. She held
out Dogger to Dave, took the big Teddy instead and went off with him
in her arms.

Then Dave smiled too.

He hugged Dogger and he hugged Bella round the waist.

"Thank you, Bella," he said.

That night Dave had Dogger in bed beside him.

Bella was practising somersaults.

"Shall you miss that big Teddy?" Dave asked her.

"No," said Bella, "I didn't like him much really. He was too big and his eyes were too staring. Anyway if I had another Teddy in my bed there wouldn't be room for me."

# Up and Up

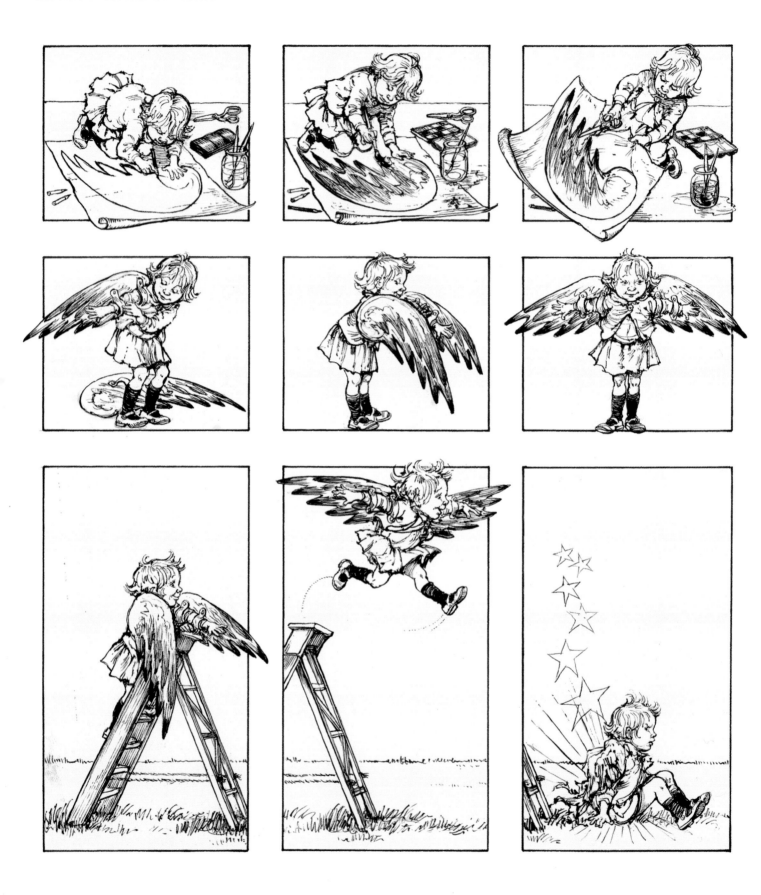

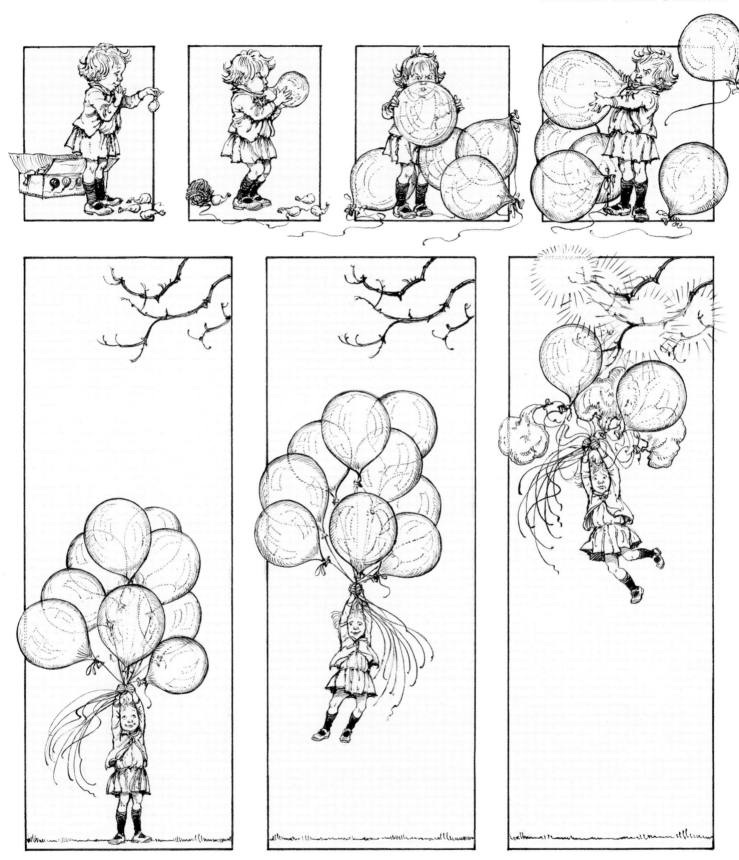

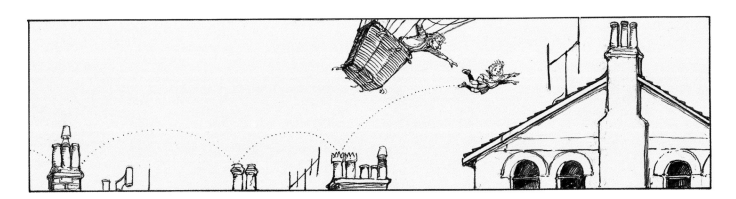

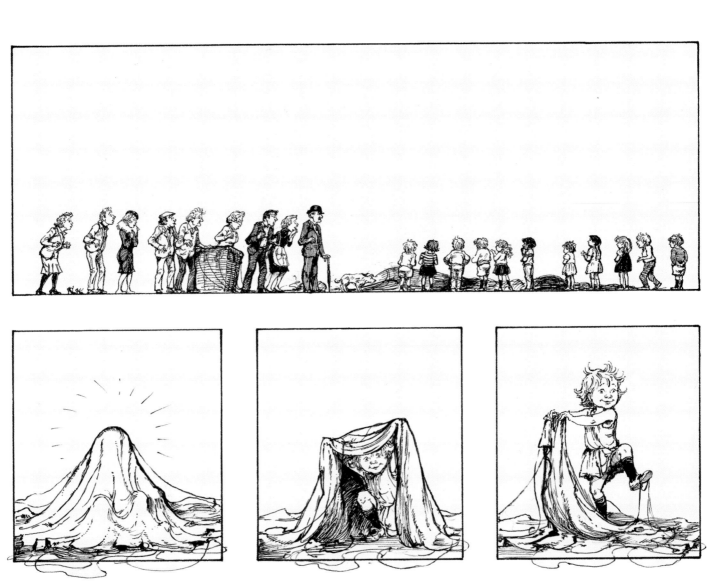

# Creepy Crawly World

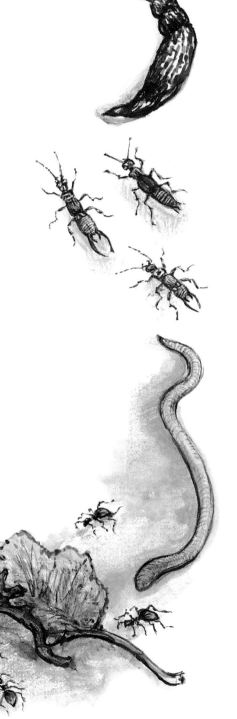

Lift up a stone and you can see
a creepy crawly world.
You can watch the creepy crawlies hurrying about,
busily moving on many legs,
with strangely shaped bodies
and feelers –
for feeling their way along.

In a creepy crawly world,
a tiny piece of twig is like a giant log
which has to be pushed,
or pulled,
or climbed over,
or patiently gone round.
Creepy crawlies don't mind how long it takes
to get where they are going.
But why they want to get there,
nobody knows.

# Alfie Gives a Hand

One day Alfie came home from Nursery School with a card in an envelope. His best friend, Bernard, had given it to him.

"Look, it's got my name on it," said Alfie, pointing.

Mum said that it was an invitation to Bernard's birthday tea party.

"Will it be at Bernard's house?" Alfie wanted to know. He'd never been 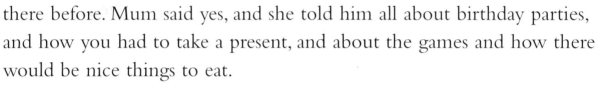 there before. Mum said yes, and she told him all about birthday parties, and how you had to take a present, and about the games and how there would be nice things to eat.

Alfie was very excited about Bernard's party. When the day came Mum washed Alfie's face and brushed his hair and helped him put on a clean T-shirt and his brand-new shorts.

"You and Annie Rose are going to be at the party, too, aren't you?" asked Alfie.

"Oh, no," said Mum. "I'll take you to Bernard's house and then Annie Rose and I will go to the park and come back to collect you when it's time to go home."

"But I want you to be there," said Alfie.

Mum told him that she and Annie Rose hadn't been invited to the party, only Alfie, because he was Bernard's special friend.

"You don't mind my leaving you at Nursery School, do you?" she said. "So you won't mind being at Bernard's house either, as soon as you get there."

Mum had bought some crayons for
Alfie to give Bernard for his birthday
present. While she was wrapping
them up, Alfie went upstairs. He
looked under his pillow and found
his old bit of blanket which he kept
in bed with him at night.

He brought it downstairs,
and sat down to wait for Mum.

"You won't want your old blanket
at the party," said Mum, when it was
time to go.

But Alfie wouldn't leave his blanket behind. He held it tightly with one hand, and Bernard's present with the other, all the way to Bernard's house.

When they got there, Bernard's Mum opened the door.

"Hello, Alfie," she said. "Let's go into the garden and find Bernard and the others."

Then Mum gave Alfie a kiss and said good-bye, and went off to the park with Annie Rose.

"Would you like to put your blanket down
here with the coats?" asked Bernard's Mum.
But Alfie didn't want to put his blanket down.
He still held on to it very tightly.

Bernard was in the garden with Min and Sam and Daniel and some other children from the Nursery School.

"Happy birthday!" Alfie
remembered to say,
and he gave Bernard
his present.

Bernard pulled off
the paper.

"Crayons! How lovely!" said
Bernard's Mum. "Say thank you,
Bernard."

"Thank you," said Bernard.
But do you know what he did
then?

He threw the crayons up in the air. They landed all over the grass.

"That was a silly thing to do," said Bernard's Mum, as she picked up the crayons and put them away.

Then Bernard's Mum brought out some bubble stuff and blew lots of bubbles into the air. They floated all over the garden and the children jumped about trying to pop them.

Alfie couldn't pop many bubbles because he was holding on to his blanket. But Bernard jumped about and pushed and popped more bubbles than anyone else.

"Don't push people, Bernard," said Bernard's Mum sternly.

One huge bubble landed lightly on Min's sleeve. It stayed there, quivering and shiny. Min smiled. She stood very still.

Then Bernard came up behind her and popped the big bubble. Min began to cry. Bernard's Mum was cross with Bernard and told him to say he was sorry.

"Never mind, we're going to have tea now, dear," she told Min. "Who would you like to sit next to?"

Min wanted to sit next to Alfie. She stopped crying and pulled her chair right up close to his.

For tea there were sandwiches and little
sausages on sticks and crisps and jellies and
a big iced cake with candles and "Happy
Birthday, Bernard" written on it.

Bernard took a huge breath and blew out all the candles at once –
*Phooooo!* Everyone clapped and sang "Happy Birthday to You".

Then Bernard blew into his lemonade through his straw and made rude bubbling noises. He blew into his jelly, too, until his Mum took it away from him.

Alfie liked the tea...but holding on to his blanket made eating rather difficult. It got all mixed up with the jelly and crisps, and covered in sticky crumbs.

After tea, Bernard's Mum said that they were all going to play a game. But Bernard ran off and fetched his very best present. It was a tiger mask.

Bernard went behind a bush and came out wearing the mask and making terrible growling noises:

"Grrr! Grrr, grrr, GRRRR! ACHT!"

He went crawling round the garden, sounding very fierce and frightening.

Min began to cry again. She clung on to Alfie.

"Get up *at once*, Bernard," said Bernard's Mum. "It's not that kind of game. Now let's all stand in a circle, everyone, and join hands."

Bernard stopped growling, but he wouldn't take off his tiger mask. Instead he grabbed Alfie's hand to pull him into the circle.

Bernard's Mum tried to take Min's hand
and bring her into the circle, too. But Min
wouldn't hold anyone's hand but Alfie's.
She went on crying. She cried and cried.

Then Alfie made a brave
decision. He ran and put down
his blanket, very carefully, in a
safe place underneath the table.

Now he could
hold Min's hand, too,
as well as Bernard's.

Min stopped crying. She wasn't
frightened of Bernard in his tiger mask
now she was holding Alfie's hand.

She joined in the game and they all
danced round together, singing:

"Ring-a-ring-o'-roses
A pocket full of posies
A-tishoo, a-tishoo,
We all fall DOWN!"

Afterwards Alfie and Min joined in with some more games and ate ice-cream and pop-corn and bounced balloons with the others. Alfie had such a good time that his blanket stayed under the table until Mum and Annie Rose came to collect him.

"What a helpful guest you've been, Alfie," said Bernard's Mum, when Alfie thanked her and said good-bye. "Min wouldn't have enjoyed the party a bit without you. I *do* wish Bernard would learn to be helpful sometimes –

Perhaps he will, one day."

On the way home, Alfie carried his blanket in one hand and a balloon and a packet of sweets in the other. His blanket had got a bit messy at the party. It had been rather in the way, too. Next time he thought he might leave it safely at home, after all.

# Birthday

Tomorrow there are going to be:
Hugs and kisses,
cards in the post,
balloons, probably,
a big cake with icing
and candles,
chocolate biscuits,
and crisps,
ice-cream,
and lots of presents.
Alfie's friends are all coming tomorrow,
and they'll all have to be
especially nice to him
because it's going to be
Alfie's Birthday!

# Bonting

One fine summer morning, Alfie went out into the back garden to look around and he found a stone. It was a specially nice sort of grey stone, worn very smooth all over with white streaks in it. It was rounded on one side and flattish on the other and it fitted well into the palm of Alfie's hand.

Alfie turned the stone over and over and passed it from one hand to the other. Then he put it into the pocket of his shorts.

He kept it there all day. Whenever
he put his hand into his pocket it
felt comforting. By the end of the
day, Alfie had decided that the
stone had become a real friend
and he called it Bonting.

Alfie liked Bonting a lot. He liked him almost as much as his blanket
and his knitted elephant. Alfie's elephant was old, nearly as old as Alfie.
But Mum said that Bonting was a lot older than that. He was very old,
perhaps thousands and thousands of years. Alfie didn't know anybody as
old as that, so it made Bonting even more special.

Mum gave Alfie a box lined with cotton-wool for Bonting to sleep in. He put it on the cupboard next to his bed.

Alfie's elephant wore a scarf and a hat to match which Grandma had knitted for him. He looked very smart in them.

Alfie asked Mum if she would please make some clothes for Bonting too. Mum said that Bonting looked as though he might be a difficult shape to fit, but she would do her best. She and Alfie looked into the basket where Mum kept her snippets of stuff and Alfie chose a bit with green and black stripes.

Then Mum made a hat for Bonting and a scarf which tied round his middle. There was a bit of stuff left over, so she made him a bathing suit as well.

The bathing suit was a good idea because the weather was getting hot.

Alfie and Annie Rose played in the back garden, splashing about in the paddling pool and sailing their toy boats. Bonting didn't float in the water. He sank straight down to the bottom and stayed there.

When Dad came home he said that if the weather stayed hot and sunny they would get up very early and drive to the seaside.

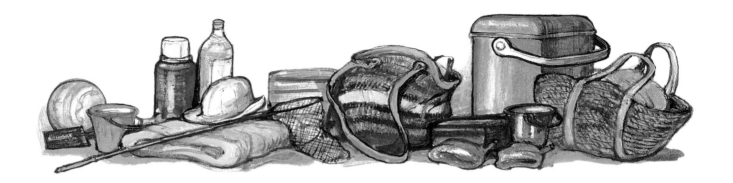

Alfie was very excited. He had seen the sea before, but that was a very long time ago and he couldn't quite remember what it looked like.

Mum got the picnic ready, and they packed up the towels and sunhats and bathing suits, and Alfie's armbands for swimming, and the buckets and spades, and put them in the car. Bonting came too, of course, inside Alfie's pocket.

It was a long drive. Inside, the car got hotter and hotter. Annie Rose went to sleep. Alfie looked out of the window hoping to see the sea, but all he could see were cars, lorries and motorbikes.

At last they arrived! The sea was huge, almost as big as the sky. It stretched away and away, full of sparkling light. Far out there were big waves. Where the sea met the beach it broke into little waves.

They arched over one another, running up the sand and then out again, sucking seaweed and pebbles with them. Alfie stood still and looked. He just couldn't stop looking.

The first thing they did was to change into their bathing suits and run
into the waves.

Then they raced each other up the beach and ate their picnic. Bonting had a little piece of Alfie's sandwich.

After lunch, Alfie gave Bonting a swim in a pool and put him carefully to dry in the sun.

Then Alfie dug a sandcastle (Dad and Annie Rose helped). And they threw a ball about.

They collected shells and bits of frilly seaweed and looked at little fish and crabs hiding in pools, under the rocks.

At last, when the tide had gone out leaving miles and miles of shining sand, and Alfie's shadow was getting longer and longer, Mum and Dad started to pack up the towels and the picnic things and get ready to go home. Alfie and Annie Rose fetched their spades and buckets full of all the special things they had collected.

Then Alfie felt in his pocket
to check that Bonting was
still there. But he wasn't! He
remembered that he had put
him out to dry after his swim.
He ran anxiously to the place
where he had left him.

But Bonting was nowhere to be seen! Alfie looked all around. There
were stones everywhere, hundreds and hundreds of them, but not one
was wearing a green and black striped bathing suit. Alfie began to be
very upset.

Of course, Mum and Dad started to look for Bonting. They hunted up and down the beach, turning over pebbles with their feet and peering into rock pools. Annie Rose hunted too. But they couldn't find him. After a long search, Dad said that it was getting so late – way past Alfie and Annie Rose's bedtime – that they really had to start for home.

"But we can't leave Bonting behind!" wailed Alfie. "He'll be all lonely on the beach at night!"

Dad put his arm round Alfie and explained that Bonting wouldn't be lonely because he would have so many other stones to keep him company. So he wouldn't mind at all.

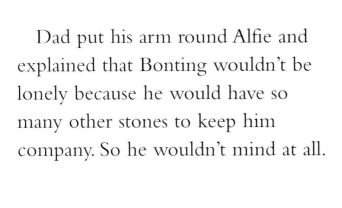

All the same, Alfie cried all the way to the car park and part of the way home in the car. In the end he was so tired that he fell asleep and so did Annie Rose.

It was very late when they arrived home. They hardly woke up when Mum and Dad carried them into the house and put them to bed.

In the morning, the first thing Alfie saw when he woke up was Bonting's empty box and he felt sad.

After breakfast, he and Annie Rose went into the back garden where Mum was hanging out the bathing suits and towels.

Their buckets and spades were by the back door. Alfie began to sort through his bucket. He had collected some lovely shells and some nice stones. He lined them up in a row on the doorstep. But none of them was quite as nice as Bonting.

Annie Rose's bucket was full of seaweed and muddy water. She picked it up and tipped out the whole lot, on to the ground. There was a strong smell of seaside.

Then Alfie and Annie Rose looked into the bottom of Annie Rose's
bucket and what do you think they saw?

It was Bonting! His green and black bathing suit was all sopping wet
and covered with mud. Alfie was *very* pleased to see him.

"Bonting will have to have a new bathing suit," he told Mum.

"His next one had better be bright
red," said Mum, "then he'll be easier
to find if you decide to take him
for another swim."

# Sea Sound

The sea, the sea!
Can you hear the sea?
Big waves like green marble,
rocking and swelling far away from land;
small splashy waves
coming in one upon another,
in long curving lines along the shore,
rushing in among the rocks,
filling up the pools
where crabs and little fishes hide.

Even when summer days are over,
and Alfie is snuggled down in his warm bed,
he sometimes puts a seashell to his ear
to hear the sea.

# Here Comes the Bridesmaid

One morning Mum had a letter from her friend Lynn, whom she used
to know at work. Lynn wrote that she was going to get married to Harvey
Jones and that she wanted them all to come to her wedding. She specially
wanted Alfie to be there because she would like him to be her page.

"What's a page?" Alfie wanted to know. "Is it something in a book?"

"No, it's not that kind of page," said Mum, still reading. "It's someone who walks behind the bride in church. There will be two big girls walking with you. They're called bridesmaids."

"But why does Lynn need all those people walking behind her, just because she's marrying Harvey Jones?" asked Alfie.

"Because on that day Lynn will be the bride and a very special person," Mum explained. "She'll wear a long white dress and you'll have to have a new shirt and a new pair of trousers."

"Is that all I have to do, just walk?" said Alfie. He didn't think that being a page sounded very interesting. But he liked Lynn and when he heard that after he'd walked behind her in church and been very good and quiet while everyone watched her get married, they would go and have a lovely party with different kinds of cake, he thought that perhaps being a page wouldn't be too bad.

The day before the wedding, Mum took Alfie down to the church to meet Lynn and the bridesmaids, so that they would all know what to do. And, of course, Annie Rose came, too. She and Mum sat at the back of the church and watched while Lynn practised walking up between all the rows of seats to the top of the church where the minister and Harvey would be standing, under a window made of coloured glass. Behind her walked Alfie, putting one foot after another very slowly and carefully, and behind him walked the two bridesmaids, side by side. Alfie had to be specially careful to leave a space between his feet and Lynn's to make room for the long dress she was going to wear.

After they'd done this a couple of times, Lynn gave Alfie a hug and told him he'd got it just right.

That evening Alfie practised some more. He made Dad walk up and down, wearing a sheet pinned round his waist and hanging down at the back, so that he could practise not treading on it. He looked hard at the ground and managed not to, not even once.

The wedding was at three o'clock the next day. Alfie and Dad, Mum and Annie Rose arrived early. Alfie, looking extra clean and tidy, stood with the two big bridesmaids at the church door, waiting for Lynn. The church was full of people. Harvey was there already, up at the front. Mum, Dad and Annie Rose sat right at the back.

At last, a big shiny car with white ribbons tied on the front drew up. Out got Lynn with her dad. She looked quite different from usual, all dressed up in her long white dress. Alfie thought she was like a princess with a crown of flowers.

Then the music played very loudly and everyone stood up. Lynn took her dad's arm and they all began to walk very slowly up the aisle to where Harvey was waiting. It was just as they had practised it, except that now all the people were looking at them. But Alfie kept his eyes straight ahead. He was being careful not to tread on Lynn's beautiful white dress.

Half way up the church, Alfie felt something behind him, tugging at the back of his shirt.

Then Alfie felt a little hand in his. It was Annie Rose! She had joined the wedding procession and was toddling happily up the church beside Alfie.

Alfie glanced round. He saw Mum looking at him, and he looked back at her. They both knew Annie Rose rather well. They knew that if Mum came and picked her up to take her back to her seat, she would scream very loudly. She might even lie down in the middle of the church and go all stiff and drum her feet on the floor. Alfie knew how terrible that would be!

So he turned round again and walked on, holding Annie Rose's hand tightly. And she walked beside him, as good as gold. She had watched him practising and knew just what to do.

When they reached Harvey and the minister, the music stopped and they all stood still. But Mum meanwhile had slipped up to the front of the church, and when Annie Rose saw her, she calmly let go of Alfie's hand and trotted over to her.

Annie Rose was very good and quiet all through the talking and singing and prayers. But when at last the wedding service was over and Lynn and Harvey walked, smiling, arm-in-arm, out of the church, Annie Rose struggled out of Mum's arms and joined in behind them next to Alfie. And she was just as careful as he was not to tread on Lynn's dress.

Outside in the sunshine the church bells rang out. Lynn and Harvey stood on the steps while a man took photographs. The bridesmaids stood on either side, and Lynn and Harvey in the middle. Then Lynn made Annie Rose stand next to Alfie, right in front, for a picture.

Afterwards they all went to a big room where a lot of beautiful food was laid out. There was a white wedding cake with a silver horseshoe on top. Alfie had two kinds of cake and some strawberries. Annie Rose had a chocolate cream roll.

"I didn't know I was going to have three bridesmaids," said Lynn, laughing. "But I guess three is a much luckier number than two!"

# People in the Street

A lot of people
live in Alfie's street.
There's Mrs MacNally
polishing her door knocker,
and Maureen,
mending her bike.
Mr MacNally
lying under his car,
with only his legs sticking out.
Here comes Gary,
whizzing up and down,
showing off his new roller-skates,
and Debbie Jones, and her mum,
going to the shop.
A lot of people go past Alfie's house:
the milkman,
and the window-cleaner,
people going to work,
and coming back.
And there's the little dog
who barks a lot,
but he's quite friendly, really
(I think).

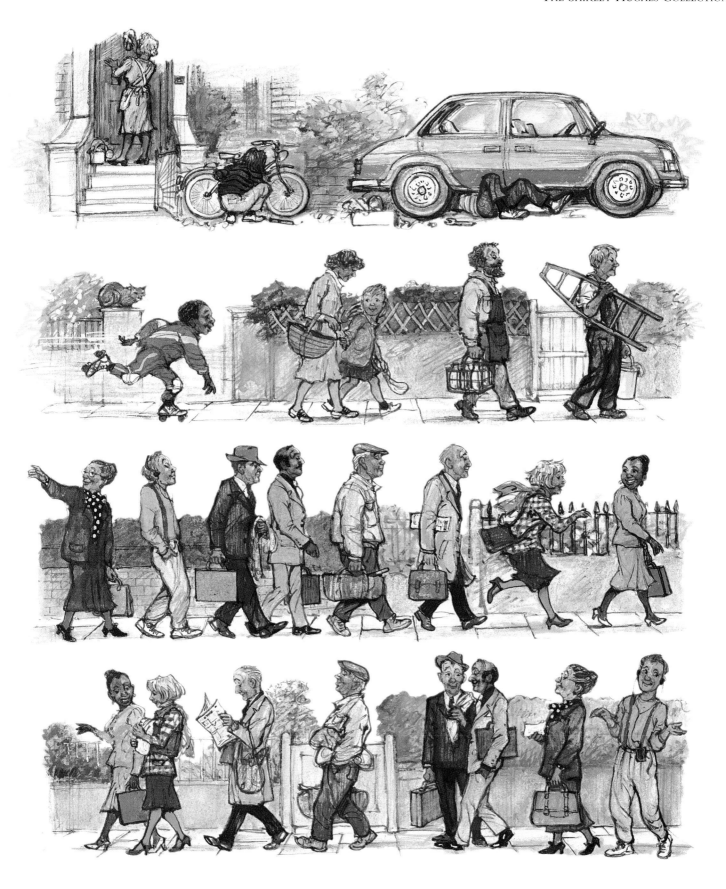

# My Naughty Little Sister at the Party

You wouldn't think there could be another child as naughty as my naughty little sister, would you? But there was. There was a thoroughly bad boy who was my naughty little sister's best boy-friend, and this boy's name was Harry.

This Bad Harry and my naughty little sister used to play together quite a lot in Harry's garden, or in our garden, and got up to dreadful mischief between them, picking all the baby gooseberries, and the green blackcurrants, and throwing sand on the flower-beds, and digging up the runner-bean seeds, and all the naughty sorts of things you never, never do in the garden.

Now, one day this Bad Harry's birthday was near, and Bad Harry's mother said he could have a birthday-party and invite lots of children to tea. So Bad Harry came round to our house with a pretty card in an envelope for my naughty little sister, and this card was an invitation asking my naughty little sister to come to the birthday-party.

Bad Harry told my naughty little sister that there would be a lovely tea with jellies and sandwiches and birthday-cake, and my naughty little sister said, "Jolly good."

And every time she thought about the party she said, "Nice tea and birthday-cake." Wasn't she greedy? And when the party day came she didn't make any fuss when my mother dressed her in her new green party-dress, and her green party-shoes and her green hair-ribbon, and she didn't fidget and she didn't wriggle her head about when she was having her hair combed, she kept as still as still, because she was so pleased to think about the party, and when my mother said, "Now, what must you say at the party?" my naughty little sister said, "I must say, 'nice tea'."

But my mother said, "No, no, that *would* be a greedy thing to say. You must say, 'please' and 'thank you' like a good polite child, at tea-time, and say, 'thank you very much for having me', when the party is over."

And my naughty little sister said, "All right, Mother, I promise."

So, my mother took my naughty little sister to the party, and what do you think the silly little girl did as soon as she got there? She went up to Bad Harry's mother and she said very quickly, "Please-and-thank-you, and thank-you-very-much-for-having-me," all at once – just like that, before she forgot to be polite, and then she said, "Now, may I have a lovely tea?"

Wasn't that rude and greedy? But Harry's mother said, "I'm afraid you will have to wait until all the other children are here, but Harry shall show you the tea-table if you like."

Bad Harry looked very smart in a blue party-suit, with white socks and shoes and a real man's haircut, and he said, "Come on, I'll show you."

So they went into the tea-room and there was the birthday-tea spread out on the table.

Bad Harry's mother had made red jellies and yellow jellies, and blancmanges and biscuits and sandwiches and cakes-with-cherries-on, and a big birthday-cake with white icing on it and candles and "Happy Birthday Harry" written on it.

My naughty little sister's eyes grew bigger and bigger, and Bad Harry said, "There's something else in the larder. It's going to be a surprise treat, but you shall see it because you are my best girl-friend."

So Bad Harry took my naughty little sister out into the kitchen and they took chairs and climbed up to the larder shelf – which is a dangerous thing to do, and it would have been their own faults if they had fallen down – and Bad Harry showed my naughty little sister a lovely spongy trifle, covered with creamy stuff and with silver balls and jelly-sweets on the top. And my naughty little sister stared more than ever because she liked spongy trifle better than jellies or blancmanges or biscuits or sandwiches or cakes-with-cherries-on, or even birthday-cake, so she said, "For me."

Bad Harry said, "For me too," because he liked spongy trifle best as well.

Then Bad Harry's mother called to them and said, "Come along, the other children are arriving."

So they went to say, "How do you do!" to the other children, and then Bad Harry's mother said, "I think we will have a few games now before tea – just until everyone has arrived."

All the other children stood in a ring and Bad Harry's mother said, "Ring O'Roses first, I think." And all the nice party children said, "Oh, we'd like that."

But my naughty little sister said, "No Ring O'Roses – nasty Ring O'Roses" – just like that, because she didn't like Ring O'Roses very much, and Bad Harry said, "Silly game." So Bad Harry and my naughty

little sister stood and watched the others.
The other children sang beautifully too,
they sang:

"Ring O'Ring O'Roses,
A pocket full of posies –
A-tishoo, a-tishoo, we all fall down."

And they all fell down and laughed,
but Harry and my naughty little
sister didn't laugh. They got tired
of watching and they went for
a little walk. Do you know where
they went to?

Yes. To the larder. To take another
look at the spongy trifle. They climbed up
on to the chairs to look at it really properly. It was very pretty.

"Ring O'Ring O'Roses," sang the good party children.

"Nice jelly-sweets," said my naughty little sister. "Nice silver balls,"
and she looked at that terribly bad Harry and he looked at her.

"Take one," said that naughty boy, and my naughty little sister did
take one, she took a red jelly-sweet from the top of the trifle; and then
Bad Harry took a green jelly-sweet; and then my naughty little sister
took a yellow jelly-sweet and a silver ball, and then Bad Harry took
three jelly-sweets, red, green and yellow, and six silver balls. One, two,
three, four, five, six, and put them all in his mouth at once.

Now some of the creamy stuff had come off on Bad Harry's fingers
and he liked it very much, so he put his fingers into the creamy stuff
on the trifle, and took some of it off and ate it, and my naughty little
sister ate some too. I'm sorry to have to tell you this, because I feel so
ashamed of them, and expect you feel ashamed of them too.

I hope you aren't too shocked to hear any more? Because, do you know, those two bad children forgot all about the party and the nice children all singing "Ring O'Roses". They took a spoon each and scraped off the creamy stuff and ate it, and then they began to eat the nice spongy inside.

Bad Harry said, "Now we've made the trifle look so untidy, no one else will want any, so we may as well eat it all up." So they dug away into the spongy inside of the trifle and found lots of nice fruit bits inside. It was a very big trifle, but those greedy children ate and ate.

Then, just as they had nearly finished the whole big trifle, the "Ring O'Roses"-ing stopped, and Bad Harry's mother called, "Where are you two? We are ready for tea."

Then my naughty little sister was very frightened. Because she knew she had been very naughty, and she looked at Bad Harry and *he* knew *he* had been very naughty, and they both felt terrible. Bad Harry had a creamy mess of trifle all over his face, and even in his real man's haircut, and my naughty little sister had made her new green party-dress all trifly – you know how it happens if you eat too quickly and greedily.

"It's tea-time," said Bad Harry, and he looked at my naughty little sister, and my naughty little sister thought of the jellies and the cakes and the sandwiches, and all the other things, and she felt very full of trifle, and she said, "Don't want any."

And do you know what she did? Just as Bad Harry's mother came into the kitchen, my naughty little sister slipped out of the door, and ran and ran all the way home. It was a good thing our home was only down the street and no roads to cross, or I don't know what would have happened to her.

Bad Harry's mother was so cross when she saw the trifle, that she sent Bad Harry straight to bed, and he had to stay there and hear all the nice children enjoying themselves.

I don't know what happened to him in the night, but I know that my naughty little sister wasn't at all a well girl, from having eaten so much trifle – and I also know that she doesn't like spongy trifle any more.

*written by Dorothy Edwards*

# Statue

When Alfie and Dad go to the park
they always see
the big stone man,
sitting high up
in his stone chair.
Down below
Alfie and Dad
chase each other
round and round,
creeping round corners
and jumping out,
Boo!
The stone man doesn't move.
He doesn't notice
even when a bird sits on his head.
At night,
when everyone's gone home
and the park's closed
and it's all dark,
he's still sitting there.

# Abel's Moon

Abel Grable was home at last. Home
from his travels, working here and
there. Home to the little house
where the gate still squeaked and
the garden was as untidy as
when he left.

Abel's wife, Mabel, and his
three children, Adam, Noah
and baby Ben, rushed to the
door to greet him. Skipper the
dog was half crazy with joy.

Abel was glad to be at home again, cosy by the
fire, telling the family about the jungles he had
camped in, where monkeys swung through the
trees overhead and crocodiles eyed him from
muddy swamps.

He told them how he had taken cargoes of
supplies by riverboat to remote places where
there were no electric lights or street lamps,
only the moon to guide the way.

Adam and Noah loved hearing about his adventures.

"Tell us again! Tell us again!" they pleaded.

Abel decided to write his stories down so he wouldn't forget. He found some paper, sat down at the old flap-top table in the spare room, sucked the top of his pen, and began to write.

But the Grables were a noisy family. Abel could hear Mabel singing along to the radio in her workroom, and Adam, Noah and Skipper playing at being wild animals in the living room below.

He came to the top of the stairs and called out: "Can you boys try to play a little more quietly please?"

Then Adam and Noah tried to play quietly. But soon they were making as much noise as before.

Now Mabel and baby Ben were dancing to
the beat. Abel put his head around the door.

"Could you turn the music down a bit,
please dear?" he asked.

"Of course, darling," said Mabel.

But when he was back upstairs, Abel
could still hear muffled giggles as they chased
each other round the room.

Abel sighed. Then he had a good idea. He folded up his table and carried it downstairs and into the garden. There he settled down to write under the apple tree. This was a splendid place to work. The noises from the house grew faint. There was only the twitter of birds overhead.

Abel wrote and wrote, filling up page after page. He wrote all day and on into the evening, when the daylight faded and the moon rose to guide his pen.

And on the very first page he wrote: "For my three noisy boys, with much love."

The stories were for them.

Soon the time came for Abel to set out again to find work.
He packed his bag, putting in his treasured photographs of
Mabel and the children.

Then they all hugged and waved goodbye.

After that the children could make as much noise as they liked.
But they missed their dad very much, especially Adam.
Wonderful letters and postcards arrived from Abel. But Adam
found it very hard to write back. There didn't seem to be much
to write about.

    They looked at Abel's postcards. And Noah made Adam read
the stories that Abel had written for them over and over again
till he knew them by heart.

The old flap-top table stayed out in the garden where Abel
had left it. It turned green with moss, and a jungle of weeds
grew up around it, so thick that you could only get into it
on hands and knees.

It was a very wild place.

Adam and Noah made their camp there. Skipper stood guard. Sometimes they were sure they could hear monkeys leaping from branch to branch in the tree above, monkeys who even threw apples down which landed – plop! – in the grass nearby.

When they had finished camping they turned the table upside
down to make a boat. And they paddled it through muddy,
crocodile-infested swamps, taking supplies to people miles
and miles away upriver with only the moon to guide them.

Then one day, Adam
had an even better idea.

He and Noah turned the table
the right way up. Adam made a
propeller and fixed it to the top.

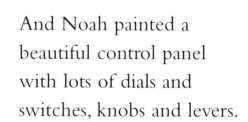

And Noah painted a
beautiful control panel
with lots of dials and
switches, knobs and levers.

Then the table wasn't an ordinary table any more.
It was a moon machine, on stand-by for take-off.

That night the moon was so bright that it woke Adam up.
It shone in at his window, seeming much closer than usual.

Adam crept out of bed
and looked down the
garden at his moon
machine. The shadow
of the apple tree moved
on it like magic.

Abel had told him once
that the moon was a cold
place and its light was
reflected from the sun.

But Adam knew better
than that. He knew that
the moon was shining down
on him, and Abel too.
It shone down on all the
people who loved each
other and couldn't always
be together, beaming
down on each and every
one, no matter how far
away they were.

And one night soon, when the moon was as bright as this, he and Noah (and Skipper if he behaved himself) might just take off in the moon machine. And they would give Abel a wonderful surprise by dropping in on him, wherever he was.

And then – it wouldn't be long now, surely – when Abel was at home once more, cosy by the fire in their little house where the gate still squeaked, and the moon machine was just an old table again, lying upside down under the apple tree –

– then they would tell him all about *their* adventures.
And Abel would listen in amazement and say:
"Tell me again, boys, tell me again. . ."

# Moon

When it's dark
Alfie likes to see the moon
up above the houses.
Sometimes it has a round face,
glittering bright,
making the sharp black shadows race across the garden.
Sometimes it's a pale, thin slice of moon,
lying on its back
and riding the clouds.

The sun is always round,
so bright that you have to screw up your eyes to look,
and shut them up again quickly.
Even then you can still see it,
floating like a penny across your eyelids.
But the moon is a silver light,
always changing,
every night a little bit different.
Magic moon.

# PART THREE

## Stories and Poems for
## Older Children

# Wild Weather

Winter is coming! The wind that blows
Hard from the north, from the land of snows,
Nips the fingers and reddens the nose
And strips the tree.

The track is sticky with mud and mire,
And crows string like crotchets along the wire,
And wanderers think of home and fire,
And so do we.

# Cinderella

Once upon a time there lived a gentleman who married, as his second wife, a handsome widow. She was however an excessively proud and ill-natured woman, and her two daughters were just like her. The man, on his side, also had a daughter, younger than her step-sisters, and she, taking after her own mother, was gentle, sweet and charming.

The wedding festivities were barely over when the woman showed her true character. She began to ill-treat her step-daughter, whose beauty and goodness made her own daughters seem all the more unattractive. The poor child was given all the rough household tasks to do. And while her step-sisters were surrounded with every comfort and luxury and lived a life of ease, the younger girl swept and dusted their rooms, washed the dishes, scrubbed the floor and steps and worked from morning till night.

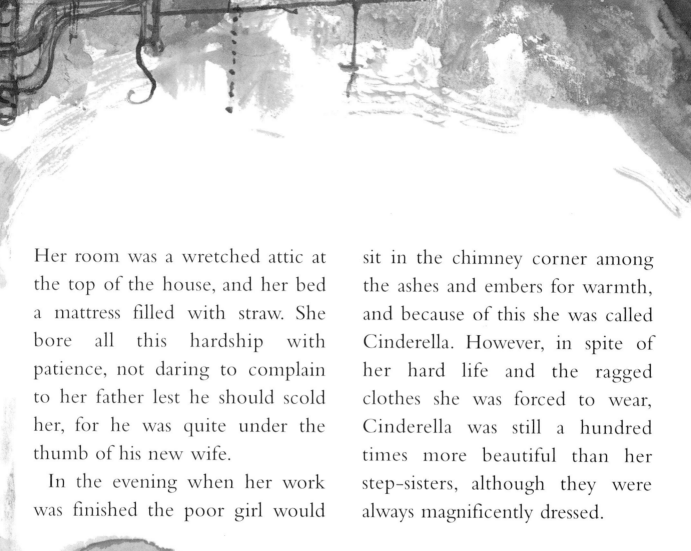

Her room was a wretched attic at the top of the house, and her bed a mattress filled with straw. She bore all this hardship with patience, not daring to complain to her father lest he should scold her, for he was quite under the thumb of his new wife.

In the evening when her work was finished the poor girl would sit in the chimney corner among the ashes and embers for warmth, and because of this she was called Cinderella. However, in spite of her hard life and the ragged clothes she was forced to wear, Cinderella was still a hundred times more beautiful than her step-sisters, although they were always magnificently dressed.

Now it happened that the king's son was giving two balls, to which all persons of fashion were invited. Of course the two young ladies received an invitation, for they went out much into society. They were delighted, and for weeks did nothing but talk about what they would wear. Cinderella was kept very busy washing and ironing and sewing for them. They ordered elaborate head-dresses from the

best milliner, and the most expensive beauty preparations.

Cinderella was called upon to help and advise them, for she had excellent taste. She arranged their hair most expertly even though they cruelly teased her, asking if she would not like to go to the balls, and saying how everyone would laugh to see a Cinderwench among the fine ladies.

At last the happy moment for departure came, and off they all went. Cinderella followed them with her eyes for as long as she could, and when they were out of sight she sat down by the fireside and burst into tears. At that moment her fairy godmother appeared beside her. "What is the matter, dear child?" she said. "Why do you cry so bitterly?"

"I wish – oh, I wish..." Cinderella began, but tears choked her and she could not go on.

"You wish that you could go to the ball, is that it?" asked her godmother.

"Oh, yes I do," sobbed Cinderella.

"Well," said the old lady, "you are a good girl and I shall see to it. Go into the garden and fetch me a pumpkin." Cinderella did as she was bid and brought the largest pumpkin she could find, but wondering all the while what use it could be. Her godmother scooped out the inside, leaving nothing but the rind, and then touched it with her wand. Instantly it became a splendid golden coach. After that she looked in the mousetrap, and found there six live mice. She told Cinderella to lift up the trap door gently and as the mice ran out one by one, she tapped each one with her wand and it was turned into a horse. So here was a team of six dapple-grey carriage horses, only needing a coachman. "I'll go and look at the rat-trap," said Cinderella, "if there is a rat in it, we'll make a coachman of him."

"You are right," said her god-mother, "go and see." There were three rats in the trap. The old lady chose the one with the longest whiskers, and at the touch of her wand, it became a fat jolly coachman with splendid moustaches. Then she told Cinderella to fetch the six lizards she would find behind the water-butt. These were changed into six footmen, wearing smart livery, who at once climbed up behind the coach as though they had done nothing else all their lives.

"There now," said her god-mother, "you have your coach and all that is necessary to go to the ball. Are you pleased?"

"Oh, yes, dear godmother," answered Cinderella. "But must I go dressed as I am in these ugly, ragged clothes?" Her godmother only just touched Cinderella with her wand, and in an instant her rags became a beautiful ball-gown made of cloth of gold and silver, and all sparkling with jewels. The old lady then gave her a pair of exquisite little glass slippers to put on. And now Cinderella got up into the coach ready to set out for the palace. But before she left, her godmother solemnly warned her to be home before the clock struck twelve. At one minute after midnight her coach would become a pumpkin again, the horses mice, the footmen lizards and Cinderella would find herself in her old clothes once more. Cinderella promised to obey her godmother, and joyfully drove off to the ball.

The prince, who had been told that an unknown princess had arrived, himself hurried out to receive her. He gave her his hand as she alighted from the coach and led her into the great hall where all the guests were dancing. When Cinderella entered the ballroom there was a moment's complete silence. Talking ceased, the dancers stood still, and the violinists stopped playing – then there was a growing murmur, "Oh, how beautiful she is, how beautiful she is." Even the old king gazed on her with delight and said softly to the queen that it was many years since he had seen such a lovely young creature. All the women carefully studied her appearance in every detail, with the intention of dressing in the same way themselves, if such materials and clever dressmakers could be found.

The prince led Cinderella to a place of honour, and later he danced with her. A splendid supper was served but the prince was so lost in admiration of her grace and beauty that he could eat nothing.

Cinderella went and sat with her sisters and was most gracious and pleasant, even sharing with them fruit that the prince had given her. This kindness astonished them for they did not recognise her. Then Cinderella heard the clock strike eleven-and-three-quarters so she got up, made a curtsey to the company and quickly left the palace.

She found her godmother waiting for her at home. After thanking her for a happy evening she pleaded to be allowed to go again to the ball next day, since the

prince had particularly asked her. While she was telling her godmother everything that had occurred, her sisters returned. The fairy vanished and Cinderella went to open the door. "You are very late," she said, yawning and rubbing her eyes, as if she had just that moment woken up; although in truth she had not for one moment during their absence thought of sleep.

"If you had been to the ball," said one of the sisters, "you would not have wished to leave any earlier. The most beautiful princess in the world was there."

"Yes," said the other, "and she sat by us and was very attentive."

Cinderella feigned indifference, but asked the name of the princess.

"No one knows," they answered, "and the king's son would give the world to find out who she is."

At this Cinderella sighed, and said, "How I wish I could see the beautiful princess."

The next evening the two sisters went again to the ball. Cinderella was there too, and was dressed even more splendidly than before. The prince was constantly by her side, paying her compliments and speaking tender words to her. He danced with no one else all evening. Cinderella was so happy that the time passed all too quickly, and she forgot her godmother's warning. The clock began to strike. It could only be eleven she thought. But it was twelve o'clock!

Cinderella jumped up and ran, swiftly as a deer. The prince followed her but did not catch her.

In her flight Cinderella dropped one of her little glass slippers, and this the prince picked up carefully and carried, while he hunted everywhere for her in vain.

The guards were questioned, but none had seen the princess leave.

Cinderella arrived home quite out of breath, without coach or footmen, and in her old clothes. Nothing was left of her finery but a little glass slipper, fellow to the one she had dropped.

When her step-sisters returned, Cinderella asked if the strange princess had been at the ball.

"Yes," they answered, "but she left as soon as the clock struck midnight, and in such haste that she dropped one of her little glass slippers. The prince has it." Then they told her that the prince must be very much in love with the owner of the slipper since he had looked at no one else the whole evening.

They spoke truly, for a few days later it was proclaimed to the sound of trumpets that the prince would marry the one whose foot the glass slipper exactly fitted. What excitement there was! The Court Chamberlain visited princesses first, and then the duchesses and after that the ladies of the court, but all to no purpose.

At last he came to Cinderella's step-sisters. Each one tried and tried to force her foot into the little slipper, but in vain. It was far too small.

Cinderella, who was watching and who knew her own slipper, said lightly, "Let me see if it will fit."

The two sisters burst out laughing and began to jeer at her. But the Chamberlain, looking at her closely, saw that she was very pretty and he said he had orders that all girls should try on the slipper and it was only right that she should have her chance. So he made Cinderella sit down and hold out her foot, and the little slipper went on easily and fitted as perfectly as if it had been moulded to her foot in wax.

The step-sisters were astonished, but they were even more astounded when Cinderella took the other slipper from her pocket and put it on. At that moment her fairy god-mother appeared,

and with a touch of her wand changed Cinderella's rags into more magnificent clothes than any she had worn before.

Then the step-sisters knew that Cinderella was the beautiful princess they had seen at the ball. They fell on their knees before her to beg forgiveness for their harsh and unkind treatment. She raised them up, and, as she kissed them, said that she forgave them with all her heart, and hoped they would always love her.

Cinderella was conducted to the prince. Their wedding took place the very next day.

Then Cinderella, who was as good as she was beautiful, brought her sisters to the palace, and soon married them to two noblemen of the court.

*written by Charles Perrault*

# Angel Mae

Mae Morgan lived with her mum and dad and her big brother Frankie in the flats on the corner of Trotter Street. Mae's grandma lived nearby. Soon there was going to be another person in the family, because Mae's mum was going to have a baby. It would be born around Christmas time.

Everyone was making preparations for the baby. Grandma was knitting little coats and booties. Dad was decorating the small bedroom. He painted the walls a beautiful yellow. Mum got out the old cradle that Mae and Frankie had slept in when they were babies. She put a pretty new lining in it.

"Imagine us being small enough to sleep in that!" said Frankie.

Mae tried sitting in the cradle. She could just fit if her knees were drawn up under her chin.

Mae thought about the baby a lot. She looked into her toy chest and pulled out some of her old toys. She was hoping to have

some lovely new things at Christmas, so she thought she would give the baby a few of her old toys.

She didn't want to give away anything too special, like her best doll, Carol. She thought she could let the baby have her old pink rabbit and the duck who nodded his head and flapped his wings when you pulled him along. And there was the ball with the bell inside it. They were all too babyish for her now.

Carefully, Mae put the rabbit, the duck and the ball into the baby's cradle.

"What are you putting those old toys in there for?" asked Frankie. "Our new baby will be much too small to play with those." And he told Mae that at first it would be a tiny little baby, not nearly big enough to play with toys. "But he might like them when he's older," Frankie said.

"How do you know it will be a he?" Mae answered crossly. Frankie said he didn't know, but he hoped it would be so he could teach the baby to play football.

Mae slowly piled up her old toys and threw them on the floor beside her toy chest.

The flat where Mae and Frankie lived was on the third floor. There were a good many stairs because there wasn't a lift. Mum got tired carrying up the shopping.

Mae got tired too. She wished she could be carried like a shopping bag.

"Carry me, carry me," she moaned, drooping on the banisters at the bottom step. But Mum couldn't carry Mae *and* the shopping. Mae was much too old to be carried anyway.

After lunch Mum sat down for a rest. Frankie put a cushion under her poor tired feet. Mae moped about. She counted Mum's toes – one, two, three, four – up to ten. Then she started to tickle her feet. But Mum didn't want her feet tickled just then. She lay back and closed her eyes but Mae knew she wasn't really asleep.

Mae went off to find Dad. He was getting ready to clean the car. He said that Mae could help if she liked, so together they went downstairs into the street. Dad gave Mae a rag so she could polish the hubcaps. Mae rubbed away until she could see her own face. It looked a bit funny.

"Do you think our baby will be a boy or a girl?" she asked.

"Nobody knows for sure," said Dad. "But as there's you and Mum and Grandma in our family already, it would even things up if it was a boy, wouldn't it?" He ruffled Mae's hair. "You'd like to have a baby brother, wouldn't you, Mae?"

But Mae said nothing. She just went on polishing.

At school, all the children were getting ready for Christmas. Mae's teacher, Mrs Foster, helped them to make paper robins and lanterns to decorate the classroom. Then Mrs Foster told everybody that they were going to act a play about baby Jesus being born. All the Trotter Street mums and dads would be invited to watch.

Nancy Jones was going to be Mary and wear a blue hood over her long fair hair and Jim Zolinski was going to be Joseph and wear a false beard. Frankie, Harvey and Billy were going to be kings. They had gold paper crowns with jewels painted round them.

Mae wanted to be a king too, but Mrs Foster said that kings were boys' parts. Mae looked into the wooden box which Mrs Foster had made into a manger for the baby Jesus. "I'll be baby Jesus, then," said Mae. She was sure she would fit into the manger if she tried very hard.

But Mrs Foster explained that they were going to wrap up a baby doll in a shawl to be baby Jesus. She said that Mae could be a cow or a sheep if she liked, but Mae certainly didn't want to be either of those. She stuck out her bottom lip and made a very cross face.

"What about being an angel?" asked Mrs Foster.

Mae didn't want to be an angel either.

"You could be the angel Gabriel," Mrs Foster told her. "That's a very special angel, a very important part."

Mae thought about this. Then she nodded her head.

"I'm going to be the angel Gave-you!" she told Frankie later.

"Angel who?" said Frankie.

"Angel Gave-you! A very special angel," said Mae proudly.

"I'm the angel Gave-you!" Mae announced, beaming, when Mum came to collect her. "Gave-you, Gave-you, Gave-you!" sang Mae as she bounced along ahead, all the way home.

"Angel Gave-you!" shouted Mae, hugging Dad round the waist when he came home from work.

"Gave me what?" asked Dad.

"Just Gave-you. That's my name in the Christmas play," Mae explained.

"Will you come and see us in it?" Frankie wanted to know.

Dad said he wasn't sure, but he would try very hard.

But when Mae and Frankie woke up on the morning of the Christmas play, neither Mum nor Dad was there! Grandma was cooking breakfast. She told them that Dad had taken Mum to the hospital in the night because the new baby was going to be born very soon.

"Will they be back in time to watch me being the angel Gave-you?" asked Mae anxiously.

"I'm afraid not," said Grandma. "But I'll be there for sure."

When Mae and Frankie arrived at school, the big hall looked very different. There was a blue curtain at one end with silver stars all over it and one big star hanging up in the middle. The smallest angels were going to stand on a row of chairs at the back. The animals were going to crouch down in front by the manger.

While the grown-ups were arriving, Mrs Foster helped the children to dress up. Mae had a white pillowcase over her front and a pair of white paper wings pinned on to the back. She was going to stand at the very end of the row because she was such a special angel.

From high up she could see all round the room. She could see all the mums and dads. Grandma was sitting in the very front row, smiling and smiling.

Then Mrs Foster sat down at the piano and all the children began to sing:

*"Away in a manger, no crib for a bed,*
*The little Lord Jesus lay down his sweet head…"*

Mary and Joseph sang, the angels sang and the animals sang. The shepherds came in and knelt down on one side of the manger. Then the three kings came in, carrying presents for baby Jesus. Mae sang very loudly.

Then she saw somebody coming in late at the very back of the room. It was Dad! He was smiling the biggest smile of all. Mae was so pleased to see him that she forgot she was in a play. She waved and shouted out, "Hello, Dad. I'm being the angel Gave-you!"

Dad put his fingers to his lips and waved back.

But Mae was waving so hard that her chair began to wobble...

and Mae wobbled too...

and then she fell right off the chair...

# Bump!

She hit the floor with a horrible crash, wings and all!

Mrs Foster stopped playing the piano. All the children stopped singing. Everyone looked at Mae. Mae held her arm where it hurt. She stuck out her bottom lip. She wanted to cry. But she didn't. Instead, she climbed up on to the chair again and went on singing:

*"The stars in the bright sky looked down where he lay,*
*The little Lord Jesus asleep in the hay…"*

Then all the people in the audience smiled and clapped a special clap for Mae for being so brave and not spoiling the play. Grandma clapped harder than anyone.

"Good old angel Gave-you!" said Dad when it was all over.

Grandma gave Frankie and Mae a hug and said it was the best Christmas play she had ever seen.

Then Dad said he had a big surprise for them. They had a new baby sister, born that morning. And Mum was going to bring her home in time for Christmas!

When Mae and Frankie went to the hospital, they looked into the cot and saw their tiny baby sister wrapped up in a white shawl. She had a funny little, crumpled up, red face and a few spikes of hair standing on end, and tiny crumpled up fingers. Mae liked the way she looked and she liked her nice baby smell. She was pleased that the baby looked so funny.

But most of all she was pleased that Mum
would be home in time for Christmas.

# Coming Soon

Spring is coming! With promising patches
Of blue; and sunlight suddenly catches
A gleaming rooftop, where sparrows in batches
Flirt and flutter and pipe up snatches
Of hopeful song;

And windows are opened on stuffy rooms,
There's a shaking of mats and a flurry of brooms,
And it's light in the longer afternoons,
And boys on bikes whistle cheerful tunes.
It won't be long!

# Sea Singing

**D**id I tell you about the time I heard singing coming from the sea? It came very high and clear, from way out beyond the rocks under the cliff. I knew it wasn't the wind or seabirds calling. It was a woman's voice, I was sure of that.

"You mustn't go near the edge, not *ever*," they had warned. "It isn't summer, remember. The wind can be very strong."

They were right, of course. They didn't need to tell me. I'm much too frightened of the rough sea, with those huge waves crashing up against the cliff and pouring and sucking over the boulders below.

I went looking in other places hoping I would hear it again, all along the beach and over the rocks at low tide. There wasn't much else to do anyway. My legs were still thin and wobbly from being ill, but I walked and walked. Sometimes I thought about my friends at home, doing proper things like going to school and shopping and watching their favourite programmes on television, and how silly they'd think me wandering about on an empty beach listening for voices.

When I told Mum's friend, Morag, about the singing, she didn't seem in the least surprised. She'd heard it herself, she said, but that was a long time ago.

I was staying with Morag, having a whole term off school. They said the sea air would do me good. Morag lives by the sea all the year round, not just for holidays. Her house is high up on the cliff. There's a room with a big window where she does her painting.

Late that afternoon Morag and I went for a walk along the cliffs. We didn't hear any singing, but the wind roared and the sky looked like a shoal of fish. Morag likes the sea best in winter.

In summertime, she told me, she has lots of visitors. They have picnics on the beach and boating parties and swim off the rocks. Morag's a very strong swimmer. "Summer is fun," she said, "and it's a wonderful thing to have friends. But I'm always quite glad when they all go home and let me get on with my painting."

Most of Morag's paintings are of the sea. Some of them she hangs up for everyone to look at. Some she stacks face up to the wall or leaves lying about on the floor. She doesn't much like people in the room with her when she's painting, but she doesn't mind me being there as long as I get on quietly with my own drawing.

Morag sings a lot while she paints. She sings along with the music on her
tapes. When she's finished she washes her brushes and makes tea and then
we talk. "I expect it was a selkie you heard singing," said Morag. Of course
I didn't know what a selkie was, so she told me.

Selkies are seal people. They can cast off their skins and take human form. Once a fisherman saw a selkie playing and sporting on the rocks with her sisters and he stole her skin so she couldn't turn back into a seal again.

That night she came crying and moaning round his cottage all running wet with her black hair dripping, begging him to give back her skin. But he wouldn't, because he wanted her for his wife.

So she stayed and was a good wife to him. She cooked for him and cleaned the house and in time they had children, two boys and a girl. She seemed happy enough and sang at her work. But often she would carry the baby with her down to the shore.

She would stand there for a long time, looking out to sea. Then a big black seal would come and swim along quite close to the tide-line. And the baby would laugh and hold out her little arms to him.

The fisherman kept his wife's skin hidden away, always changing it to a different place so that she couldn't find it. But sometimes he would relent and let her hold it, just for a little while. One day, when she held it in her hands, she tricked him into thinking that something was wrong with the sheep on the hillside.

He hurried up there to see, but found nothing amiss. When he got back his wife was gone. The little boys were safe inside the cottage. They told him that their mother had taken the baby down to the sea. Panic stricken, he ran off down the cliff path, shouting her name into the wind.

He found his baby daughter playing happily on the shore. His wife's clothes were lying on a rock nearby. When he asked her where her mother was, she pointed out to sea. He picked her up and ran along the beach, calling and calling. But when darkness fell he gave up hope and went back to care for his family alone.

The selkie wife never came back to live with them again. But sometimes, in the morning, he would find wet footprints on the floor around the children's beds and their pillows damp with salt water. One night he lay in wait and the selkie appeared, crying over her children and kissing them as they lay asleep.

Then he lit the candle and told her how desperately he missed her and wanted her back. She replied sadly that she could never return. She told him that she had a seal-husband and other children in the sea, and that she belonged there with them.

That's really the end of the story. From that time on the fisherman just had to live without his selkie wife. Perhaps he had always half known that one day she would go back to the sea. But on the children's birthdays there were always presents — coral beads and combs and wonderful mother-of-pearl boxes — left on that same rock by the shore.

"How do you know all this about selkies?" I asked Morag when she had finished the story.

She just smiled and said, "My grandmother told me."

Soon I was strong again and it was time for me to say goodbye to Morag. She gave me one of her pictures to take home with me.

It's very beautiful, all watery and curving. I have it on my bedroom wall.

Sometimes I think it looks like waves, or the shape of a seal, or perhaps a woman swimming. Sometimes, when I look at it for a long time, I think it looks like Morag herself, with her hair spreading like dark weed on the water.

# The By-Gone Fox

Chips' mum had been asked to run a stall at the Church Bazaar on Saturday. Grandpa was going to look after Gloria, and Chips and Jessie were going to be helpers. They were going to sell By-Gones.

All week Mum collected up the By-Gones which people gave her for the stall. Chips didn't think much of them.

Before the Bazaar began Chips and Jessie were busy helping Mum arrange the stall. Quite a crowd of people were waiting to come in when the doors opened. Some of them stopped to look at the By-Gones. One or two of them even bought something.

Next to the By-Gones was a secondhand clothes stall. This was a big attraction. Winston's mum was doing a brisk trade. Winston was there, too, getting in her way.

Mrs Sharp, the school janitor's wife, arrived all dressed up in her fox fur, and made a bee-line for the secondhand clothes stall. She was an old enemy of Chips. She and her friend were looking for a bargain. Mrs Sharp couldn't make up her mind which coat suited her best. She thought she liked the blue one.

She took off her fur and
laid it over a chair. Then she
and her friend became very
absorbed in discussing whether
or not the blue coat fitted,
while Winston's mum made
encouraging remarks.

Mrs Sharp turned this way and that
in front of the mirror. She didn't
notice when somebody moved her
fur from the chair and put it down
among the By-Gones. Neither did
anyone else.

At this point Grandpa appeared,
pushing Gloria in the buggy.
Grandpa was having a difficult
afternoon. Gloria was in one
of her bad moods. She sat in
her buggy, grizzling steadily.

When Gloria saw Mum she started to yell. She arched her back, kicked her legs about and tried to get out of her buggy.

I can't seem to do anything with her!

Oh dear, it's her teeth again, I suppose.

Mama!

Can't you give her a drink or something?

I think you'll have to come with us and try to settle her down.

Waah!

So Mum and Grandpa took Gloria off in search of an orange-juice to cheer her up, and a cup of coffee for themselves. Chips and Jessie were left in charge of the By-Gones.

They had strict instructions to write down every sale while Mum was away. Jessie sold a cracked jug with a picture of swans on it. Chips tried very hard to sell an old clock.

It isn't going at the moment, but perhaps it will when you get it home...

You could always stick on another minute hand.

A young lady was hovering round the stall, idly picking over the things. Her eye fell on Mrs Sharp's fox fur.

When she asked the price, Chips promptly told her two pounds. It was the first sum which came into his head.

The young lady put the fur over her shoulder with the head and front paws hanging down the front, looking very foxy indeed. She stroked the fur. Luckily she was hardly listening to Chips' eager sales-talk.

"I think I'll take it," said the young lady. She handed Chips two pound notes from her purse and went off into the crowd with the fox fur draped over her shoulder. Chips was very pleased with himself.

Mrs Sharp had by this time tried on five different coats and decided against them all. She turned round to collect her fur and found it had gone! She was not the sort of person to avoid making a fuss. What was more, she had a very loud voice.

She set up a great hue and cry, saying that her fur had been stolen. Chips turned scarlet in the face when he realised what had happened. He looked round desperately for the young lady, but she seemed to have disappeared completely.

Chips plunged into the crowd, leaving Jessie to look after the By-Gones. Mrs Sharp walked off in a rage. She and her friend were going to ask the Vicar to make an announcement on his loudspeaker.

Things looked bad. But fortunately, at that very moment, Jessie looked up and saw the young lady. She had come to ask for her money back! She had decided that she didn't much like wearing a fur with paws and a foxy face, after all.

Jessie was delighted. She quickly gave the young lady her two pounds back. Then she called out to Chips, holding the fur high above her head in triumph. Chips was so relieved that he rushed up and started to dance a foxtrot with it round the By-Gones stall. But Jessie seized it from him and hurried off.

She was just in time to return it to Mrs Sharp before the Vicar made his announcement.

"Where did you find it, then?" Mrs Sharp asked Jessie, suspiciously. Her eyes were as beady as the ones on her fox fur. Jessie explained that it had been put on the By-Gones stall by mistake.

Mrs Sharp whisked her fur round her neck and went off, very huffily, with her friend. The Vicar was pleased. He told Jessie that she had saved the afternoon. He said that she and Chips and Winston had done so well that they could finish up all that was left on the home-made cake and sweet stall when the Bazaar was over. Which wasn't a bad ending to a foxy tale.

# Part Four

Stories for all to enjoy

# Enchantment in the Garden

Once, in an old Italian city, in a house with many rooms, there lived a girl called Valerie. The front of the house faced severely on to the street. At the back, balconies overlooked a shady garden with stone seats, a goldfish pond and plant pots overflowing with flowers.

There was also a smaller house where Pietro, the gardener, and his wife, Maria, lived. And beyond that, over a high wall, lay a great public garden which had once belonged to a merchant prince. It was full of statues. Valerie could just see some of their heads from the balcony of her bedroom.

Valerie's father was a rich man. He owned hotels and restaurants all over Italy and was often away from home. Her mother was a beautiful American lady. She breakfasted late, long after Valerie had started her lessons, then drove out to meet her friends. In the evening she put on an elegant dress covered in sparkling beads and went to balls and parties.

In between whiles she spent a lot of time lying on the sofa in the lofty salon. Sometimes she and Valerie had tea together and played dance records on the gramophone.

Valerie was an only child. She was too serious for her age and had more toys and dresses than she could possibly need. But she had few friends and, of course, she was lonely.

Every day in the late afternoon, Valerie and her governess, Miss McKenzie, set out for the garden – through the cool gravel walks then out by the sunlit lake where Neptune, the great sea god, rode on a sea monster surrounded by nymphs.

Valerie's favourite statue of all was a beautiful long-haired boy who rode on a dolphin. Clear water poured from its open jaws. When Valerie gazed at them, how she longed to take off her clothes too and splash about in the lake. But Miss McKenzie would never have allowed it.

One afternoon, when Miss McKenzie was sitting on one of the stone seats with her eyes tightly closed (she could sleep sitting bolt upright), Valerie slipped away.

The gardens around the lake were empty. The boy on the dolphin stood alone. Valerie climbed on to the curved wall which ringed the water and put out a hand to stroke his cold cheek. Then she put her face close to his ear and whispered: "You are my best friend. I love you and I am going to give you a name." And she sprinkled a little water over the boy's head. "I christen you Cherubino," said Valerie, solemnly.

The boy looked back at her. She thought she saw a dancing spark in his carved eyes.

The next day when Valerie and Miss McKenzie arrived at the gardens, they found a small crowd gathered near the lake. The dolphin was there as usual. But the boy was gone.

"Stolen!" cried the park keeper. "Thieves! Vandals! Someone has been in the night and taken one of our valuable statues!"

The crowd murmured angrily and the police were summoned. Miss McKenzie, tut-tutting, hurried Valerie away.

Valerie ran ahead of her, dodging through the maze of walks. She desperately wanted to be on her own. But when at last she thought she was out of sight, she heard a scuffling behind the hedge, keeping pace with her.

The sound of bare feet. She could see something moving behind the leaves. She had a sense of being watched; as though the statues were stealthily turning their eyes to look down at her. She ran faster.

Now she came to an open space. And there, suddenly, into a shaft of sunlight, stepped Cherubino! He was holding out his arms to her and laughing.

"Cherubino! You're alive!" cried Valerie, as she ran forward to clasp his hands.

There was no time to say any more. Miss McKenzie came hurrying in from another entrance and then, what a fuss! You never saw such a commotion. A boy in the gardens with next to no clothes on. Whatever next?

People came running. They covered Cherubino with scarves and coats and hustled him away, scolding and bombarding him with questions.

Nobody paid the least attention to Valerie as she ran behind, pulling Miss McKenzie

with her and shouting out: "But he's Cherubino, I tell you! He's one of the gods of the garden!"

No one could decide what was to be done with Cherubino. A search was made for parents or relatives, but none could be found. When he tried to explain that he was more than two thousand years old and had been carved out of Greek marble, naturally, nobody believed him.

In the end, they took him to an orphanage and put him in the care of the nuns, in the hope that he would be cured of telling such wicked lies.

The orphanage was on the other side of the city. There was no garden, only a gloomy yard with high walls, where the sunlight hardly ever ventured. They cut off Cherubino's hair and dressed him in a uniform; a grey cotton shirt and clumsy black boots like the other boys. He was given a narrow iron bed in a bleak dormitory and he no longer laughed. Very soon he fell completely silent.

No matter how hard they tried, the nuns could not get him to eat the black bread and watery stew they provided. After some weeks Signor Duro himself, the chief governor of the orphanage, had to be summoned. He quickly came to the conclusion that Cherubino was wilfully fading away.

Meanwhile Valerie, usually such an obedient and even-tempered child, was creating a terrible fuss. She too refused her meals and lay on her bed weeping. Several expensive doctors were summoned. But all Valerie could say was: "We must find Cherubino!" At last her mother, seriously worried, made inquiries as to the whereabouts of this mysterious boy.

Pietro was given orders to bring the car round and drive Valerie and her mother across the city to the orphanage. They found Cherubino standing in line with the other boys. His shoulders drooped pathetically, as though the weight of his braces was too heavy for him, and his cheeks were pale and thin.

When Valerie saw him she let out a cry of joy, flung her arms around him and refused to be separated. So it was that Valerie's mother offered Cherubino a home.

It was arranged that he would come and live with Pietro and Maria, who were childless, and learn to be a gardener's boy. As soon as he was settled and could see Valerie every day, Cherubino's health improved.

He began to eat ravenously and his cheeks became rosy and brown from working out of doors. To everyone's delight he turned out to be a natural gardener. Seedlings

prospered and flowers bloomed under his hands.

He worked hard, became cheerful, high spirited and hilariously merry. He drove Pietro to distraction, but the cats loved him.

Often he and they put on a great show for Valerie, who watched giggling from her balcony. He always finished with an elaborate bow to a wildly enthusiastic, imaginary audience.

At this time, rich children were not supposed to become friendly with servants. Miss McKenzie certainly would not allow it. But in the evening, when the governess was listening to her wireless set, Valerie climbed down from her balcony to meet Cherubino. Hidden behind the shadowy vines they whispered and laughed together and, more often, talked seriously until late into the night. Little by little Valerie learned Cherubino's story. How, thousands of years ago – even before he had become a statue – he had been alive in the morning of time. His father was a sea god who ruled the ocean, with the strength of all the tides in his limbs and forked lightning in his beard. He had fallen in love with Cherubino's mother, a human woman, and she had brought Cherubino up in her own country; a beautiful fertile place, rich with fruits and golden grain, in what was now called North Africa.

But then Valerie, remembering her geography lessons with Miss McKenzie, fetched her atlas and showed Cherubino that this part of the world was now dry desert, where only goats and camels could find enough to eat. At first he refused to believe it. Then he flew into a terrible rage and ran off.

He climbed over the wall and disappeared into the gardens. They could not find him for two whole days.

After this, Cherubino became restless. He still worked hard at helping Pietro, but he no longer wanted to laugh or fool around, or talk with Valerie late into the night. He spent his spare time sitting perfectly still by the little pond, glaring at the goldfish gliding to and fro under the lily leaves.

When Valerie asked him what was wrong, he only muttered: "The sea, the sea! I must go to the sea!" Under the suntan he had become quite pale with desperation.

The weather was growing hotter and hotter. The city was becoming unbearably dusty. By midday all the grown-ups lay prostrate behind closed shutters, to avoid the sun's fierce, wide-open eye.

Valerie's father owned one of the largest and most splendid hotels on the Italian coast. Valerie's mother always took her there for a month in the summer. Somehow, Valerie persuaded her to let Cherubino come too.

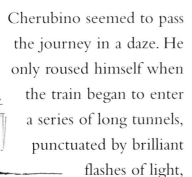

Of course, there was the usual great production of packing and preparation before they boarded the train for Porto Azzurro.

Cherubino seemed to pass the journey in a daze. He only roused himself when the train began to enter a series of long tunnels, punctuated by brilliant flashes of light, tantalising glimpses of sunlit beaches and clear green water. The sea – at last, the sea!

Porto Azzurro was the smartest resort on the whole Italian Riviera. Their hotel was a great white palace, set among palm trees and lush foliage, its domes and pinnacles melting into the blue haze.

At the steps to the main entrance, Cherubino stopped. He stood stock still and refused to move. A shadow crossed his face. Only Valerie noticed.

While Miss McKenzie was fussing with the luggage, Valerie slipped over to

Cherubino's side and took his hand. "Let's go down to the sea!" she whispered. And together they ran.

They reached the paved esplanade and looked down on a beach, alive with people.

Cherubino stood and watched them. He was as still as the statue he had once been. "It's the sea, Cherubino – aren't you glad to see it?" asked Valerie.

Cherubino looked at the polite waves lapping on to the sugary sand. He did not reply. Instead he let out a wild cry of anger and pain. Then he was off, kicking up sand, skidding through carefully laid picnics, trampling on wet towels, sending hats, sandcastles and sunshades flying. "Come back! Come back!" called Valerie. But she knew it was hopeless. She watched Cherubino run out of sight, then walked back alone to the hotel and waited furiously until bedtime.

But Cherubino did not return.

That night the weather changed. A great storm broke. Forked lightning and thunderbolts cracked across the sky. Towering waves pounded and raked the esplanade, throwing deckchairs and beach umbrellas about like matchwood.

When at last morning came, the sky was still dark and threatening and a strong wind blew in relentlessly from the sea. There was still no sign of Cherubino. Now everyone began to be worried. A search party was organised, but Valerie was not allowed to join in. Her anger at Cherubino had turned to a terrible anxiety. She waited alone in the huge, glass-fronted winter garden of the hotel, staring out at the rain which fell as steadily as her tears.

The search went on for three days. In the end it was declared hopeless. Cherubino had run away they said, or perhaps even been drowned. Some of them seemed to be more irritated than sad.

Valerie's mother ordered the luggage to be re-packed. The weather was so bad there was little point in staying, she said.

"But what if Cherubino comes back to the hotel, trying to find us?" asked Valerie.

"They'll let us know. You mustn't fuss, darling," was all her mother answered.

Back in the city, the grown-ups were out of sorts and Valerie was miserable. She missed Cherubino more than she could say and wandered around the house and garden fretting over what might have happened to him.

Weeks passed.

Then, one night, Cherubino came back.

Everyone in the house was asleep, when Valerie was woken by tiny pebbles thrown against her shutters.

She crept out on to her balcony and saw Cherubino standing there in the hot, still garden. The moon was making shadows ripple all over him like water.

Valerie was joyful when she saw him. She slipped quietly downstairs and out of the garden door.

"Cherubino, where ever have you *been*?"

"To the sea, of course," answered Cherubino, clasping her hands tightly. "But – oh Valerie; it's so different from what I remember – so changed! All those hotels and villas and *motorcars*!"

"They are there so that people can enjoy themselves," Valerie told him.

"But people don't *own* the sea any more than the fish who swim in it do," said Cherubino. "They shouldn't be so greedy. That's why I made the storm," he added, carelessly.

"Don't be *silly*, Cherubino," whispered Valerie. "Boys can't make thunder and lightning and things of that sort on purpose."

Cherubino plunged his hands into the pockets of his ragged trousers and drew himself up proudly.

"I can," he said. "I am not a boy, remember. I am the son of a sea god and

I am thousands of years old! I was inside the statue until you rescued me. But now I have come to say goodbye!"

This made Valerie's eyes fill with tears, but she was too brave to cry. Instead she told Cherubino, all in a great breathless rush, about her own plans. How she did not intend to grow up like her mama and spend all her time dressing up and going to parties. Instead she was going to study all the mysteries of the oceans.

"Wait for me…stay here until I'm older…then we can explore the wild seashore together – you and me!"

But Cherubino shook his head. "I have to go now!" he said. "I was the god of the garden, but now I must follow my father and be a god of the sea. I must guard the wild places. And I will walk in the country where I was born, which has become a dry desert, until it is green and fertile once more!"

"Then I'll never see you again," said Valerie, very quietly.

"Oh yes of course you will," answered Cherubino. "We'll meet in the remote places, in the deep sea caverns, by the rocks at high tide."

He clasped Valerie's hands again, but his touch was curiously cold, like marble. The moonlight was still playing over him but now it was making him flicker like lightning.

He led Valerie to the high wall which overlooked the great garden beyond. The tops of the statues glimmered among the dense hedges. All at once Cherubino was on top of the wall looking down at her.

He looked very grand and beautiful.

"I won't tell anybody," said Valerie, "about you being a sea god, I mean. Not even Mama. And certainly not Miss McKenzie. She would never understand!"

Cherubino was poised to jump.

Then he turned back.

"By the way, sea gods can love humans sometimes, you know. Now and again – every thousand years or so. A very unusual human that is. And when we do, we have very long memories. Goodbye, Valerie, till we meet again."

A cloud came over the moon. When it passed, Cherubino was gone.

Valerie stood there trembling for a long time. At last she remembered that she was out in the garden in her nightdress, in the middle of the night. Very slowly she went back indoors and upstairs to bed. She lay wide awake, staring into the darkness.

After this, life went on as usual; the flat days, the stifling routine. Nobody guessed that inside Valerie's head everything was different. She did her morning lessons with Miss McKenzie, as before, and in the afternoons they took their walk in the gardens.

One day they found that a change had been made. Cherubino's dolphin had disappeared. In its place was a graceful nymph with bound-up hair and trailing seaweed. She was very beautiful, but Valerie could not bear to look at her. It was a hot afternoon.

When Miss McKenzie was settled on her favourite seat and, still sitting primly upright, had fallen into a light doze, Valerie escaped.

She wandered all alone (Mama would never have approved) through the maze of shaded walks, which criss-crossed one another like a giant's ruled-out pattern book, venturing further than ever before.

High up, where the last hedge of the gardens met the steep hillside, the paths became more overgrown.

There was a flight of shallow stone steps, now cracked and neglected, with a channel running down the centre where water had once tumbled. Now the fountain at the top was dried up and covered with moss and ferns. Valerie climbed the steps and peered into the shade beyond.

This was where the gardeners tipped their grass cuttings and stacked the plant pots and cracked urns. Scattered in the long grass were bits of statues, stone legs and arms, grinning dragons split apart by time and heads of Roman emperors who had long since lost their bodies. And there, dumped down high and dry among them, was the dolphin. He seemed lonely and abandoned, but he was still smiling his wide dolphin smile.

Valerie hurried over and knelt down in front of him. She stroked his domed forehead and ran her fingers along his wide jaws. She looked into his stone eyes and he looked back at her.

It was a meeting of long lost friends. And for the first time in so many dreary days, Valerie smiled.

It was as though they both knew for sure, now, that they were going to find Cherubino again. Or, he would find them.

Somewhere, where remote caverns fill up with lapping water at high tide, and spray foams against the rocks, and breakers roll in endlessly along the beach, and the shining swell is moving, moving far out towards the sky…There, one day, as Cherubino had promised, they would meet again.

# It's Too Frightening For Me!

**D**own by the railway footpath, quite near to where Jim and Arthur lived, was a big house. It was a gloomy old place with high brick walls. The windows were boarded up and the gates always kept padlocked. Nobody went in and nobody came out, except for a big tom cat, as black as a shadow.

On one of the gateposts, carved in stone, was the name: HARDLOCK HOUSE.

There were spooks in there. Jim and Arthur knew this for sure because they had heard the ghostly screams.

Sometimes they dared one another to squeeze through the gate, where the bars had rusted away, and creep up the overgrown drive. Thick bushes grew on either side, dripping and rustling.

Round the corner, the drive opened out into a bit of garden where a crumbling porch tottered over the front door. There were little windows on either side of it with cracked panes of coloured glass. But Jim and Arthur never got a closer look before the screaming started, high and shrill.

"Go away, go away, go awayeeeeeee…" it screamed.

Jim and Arthur never waited to find out what was going to happen next.

"It's a spook!" little Arthur would say, his eyes wide with fright. "There's a horrible witch in there. Don't let's *ever* go there again, Jim."

GASP!

Run for it, Arthur!

But somehow neither of them could keep away for long.

Arthur had some nasty thoughts about the house in his bed at night. Jim always pretended not to mind about that sort of thing.

One day in the holidays, when they were messing about on the railway footpath behind Hardlock House, they spotted a foothold in the high brick wall at the back of the house. Jim gave Arthur a leg up and climbed after him.

They both sat astride the wall looking over some outhouses to the high windows beyond.

All was quiet. One of the windows was unshuttered.

Suddenly a white face appeared, looking out at them! It was a young girl.

They stared at each other silently.

Then she beckoned, and was gone.

Jim and Arthur sat for a long time staring up at the empty window. Then they slid down on to the footpath and sat with their backs against the wall.

"Arthur," said Jim seriously, "that wasn't a spook. It was a girl. This is a real mystery."

"Yes," said Arthur. "*But it's too frightening for me!*"

Jim was frightened too, but he didn't let on to Arthur.

Jim's and Arthur's Mum had once read them a story about a girl who was shut up in a tower by a wicked witch. They thought a great deal about the face at the window of Hardlock House.

Next day they watched from the wall
for a long time, but no face appeared.
Then Jim noticed a basement door at
the bottom of a flight of steps, where
the shutter had slipped and a glass pane
was broken.

Jim slithered down into the yard and
tried the door. It opened! Putting his
finger to his lips, Jim made signs to
Arthur to stay where he was. Then he
disappeared into the house.

Poor Arthur! He badly wanted to
run home, but he couldn't desert his
brother. After a long while, he too
climbed softly down into the yard and,

trembling all over, crept in through
the basement door to look for Jim.

Inside the house was a long
passage, smelling unpleasantly
of damp. There were empty
storerooms on either side, with
high, barred windows which let
in a little dreary light.

Up a shadowy flight of stairs
and into a large hall crept Arthur,
expecting to be pounced upon at
any moment.

There were a great many doors
leading off the hall. Arthur paused.
He heard voices.

He peeped through the crack in one of
the doors. Then he opened it a tiny bit,
and a little wider, and peered round...

...and there, as large as life, was that
cheeky Jim! He was sitting on the floor,
in a room full of furniture muffled in
dust-sheets, talking to the fair-haired girl.
He had forgotten all about Arthur!

Arthur felt like punching Jim but he
couldn't because Jim was bigger than
he was.

Besides, he wanted to find out about
this girl. She looked rather nice, though
a little skinny. She was certainly not a spook.

Jim started to explain. "This is Mary,
and she..."

But at this moment the terrible ghostly
screaming was heard in the hall. It was
just outside the door!

In rushed a bony figure, all in
black with wild white hair, waving
its stick-like arms about and
gobbling like a goose in between
the screams.

"Go away - AAAAH - go
away - SHRIEK - I'll have no
lads in here - AAAAUGH, gobble,
gobble, gob - get out, GET OUT!!"

Jim and Arthur both dived under
a dust-sheet and crouched there,
like a couple of ghosts themselves.

They were trapped.

But Mary was speaking calmly.

"Come on, Gran, behave yourself. What about a nice cup of tea, then?"

It wasn't a witch. It was Mary's Granny, but she was very nearly as frightening. Peeping
out from their sheet, Jim and Arthur saw Mary take her hand.

Slowly the screaming stopped. Mary managed to coax the old lady down to the kitchen
and sat her in her chair. Not knowing quite what to do, Jim and Arthur followed, and stood
about sheepishly.

While Granny sipped her tea,
still gobbling and mumbling into
her cup, Mary explained that she
was having one of her 'turns'.
She always had them when
anyone came near the house.
She couldn't stand visitors,
because she mistook them for
people from the Council
coming to ask questions and make her fill in difficult forms. This set her off in a screaming
fit. She never went out, and didn't like Mary to go out either. Even the grocery man had
to leave their boxes of food at the gate.

Mary told Jim and Arthur that she and Granny had come from far away in the country to be caretakers at Hardlock House. They had found the job through an advertisement. The owner of the house, Captain Grimthorpe, was never there. In fact, Granny had only seen him once, though a painting of him hung in the hall in a big gold frame. He looked very grand, with bushy ginger hair and whiskers.

*We're too poor to look after things properly*

Now he had gone off abroad and it seemed he had forgotten all about them, for he never sent any money for repairs. It was very worrying.

Mary was an orphan. She and Granny had only each other in all the world. Although they loved each other very much, Mary was bored and lonely without friends of her own age. School hadn't begun yet, and there was nothing to do but to sit at the window and watch the trains go rattling by. Her only companion was the black cat, Uriah. She begged Granny to let Jim and Arthur come and see her sometimes.

*Please, Gran, I do so need some friends*

Granny was reluctant at first, but finally she agreed. After this the three children often played together, and Mary learnt lots of new games. She was specially good at football.

Sometimes Jim and Arthur even offered to help Granny sweep up, and went round trying to mend things for her.

*IT'S A GOAL!*

One afternoon they found Mary and Granny
both in tears. It was over Mary's clothes. She
had to wear grown-ups' old ones, cut down
for her by Granny.

"How can I go to a new school in
these things?" sobbed Mary. "All the
other children will laugh at me."

Jim and Arthur thought it strange to cry
over a thing like clothes. But they had to
admit that, although Granny had done
her best, Mary didn't look quite like

other girls. Her skirts were too long and limp, and her shoes looked
funny. They decided to see what they could do.

That evening Jim and Arthur emptied out their money-boxes. They found
that they had £2.83 between them. They asked their Mum if she knew
where they could get some nice girl's clothes, very cheap. Mum was
a sensible lady and didn't ask too many questions.

A few days later she produced a large
box full of second-hand clothes
which had been given to her
by a rich friend. Jim and
Arthur, for their part, managed
to buy a parcel of assorted hats
for 50p at the local jumble-sale.
Some of them seemed just a
little unsuitable.

But when they arrived at
Hardlock House with all these
things, Mary was so delighted
that she put on as many as
possible all at once, and danced
about the room in them.

Jim and Arthur were so pleased with themselves. Even Granny cheered up a bit.

GRRRRRR

It was a lovely afternoon.

"I think Mary's my very best friend," Arthur told Jim as they strolled up the drive the following evening.

"Even her Gran's not such a bad old thing really, when you get used to her," added Arthur.

But a terrible shock was in store for them. As they turned the bend, they stopped short in front of the lighted window ahead. Against the closed blind was the shadow of an enormous man!

Jim and Arthur didn't know quite what to do. After a while they went round to the back door and knocked timidly. Immediately there was a great noise of barking and the door was flung open by a fat man with ginger curls and whiskers, holding a villainous-looking red-eyed dog on a lead.

Behind him in the passage they could see Mary and Granny, clinging together.

"What the devil do you want?" the man shouted. "I won't have boys knocking at my door! Take yourselves off before I set the dog on you!"

Jim and Arthur were too surprised to do anything but obey.

The next day they hung about on the footpath until at last Mary put her head over the wall. She looked unhappy and had been crying.

She told them that the owner of the house, Captain Ginger Grimthorpe, had returned suddenly. He was very cross about the state of the place, and was threatening to send them away. Then they would be homeless! What was more, he did nothing but shout at them, and his dog kept barking at Uriah.

Now Jim and Arthur were never allowed to see Mary. She had very little chance to play anyway, as she had to spend so much time doing housework and helping Granny look after Captain Grimthorpe. He was very demanding and sat about grumbling all day.

Poor Granny was quite worn out with all the work, and running up and down stairs.

But worse was to come.

Uriah had a big fight with Captain Grimthorpe's red-eyed dog.

He chased him all over the house and scratched him badly on the nose.

Captain Grimthorpe said that he wouldn't have that badly-behaved cat about the place any longer, and he locked Uriah in an upstairs room.

He was to be sent away to a Cats' Home in the morning!

Jim and Arthur looked very grave when they heard this news. They liked Uriah very much, as he was such a jolly good fighter.

"Don't worry," said Jim, "we'll save him somehow."

He was a very resourceful boy.

Together they thought of a plan. Mary was to get the key of the room in which Uriah was imprisoned. This was difficult, as it hung on a hook in the hall, just outside Captain Grimthorpe's sitting-room.

But Captain Grimthorpe always ate and drank too much at supper-time, and went off to sleep in a chair with his mouth open. The red-eyed dog did the same, stretched out on the rug. Neither of them heard Mary as she slipped gently into the hall, took the key, and crept upstairs.

The plan was to put Uriah into a cat basket, and lower him out of the window
on a long rope, to the boys who would be waiting in the yard below.

Uriah was very pleased to see Mary, and greeted her with loud purring.
But he didn't like the look of the cat-basket at all.

It was a terrible job to get him to go into it. At last the lid was safely
tied down.

Leaning out, Mary could see Jim's and Arthur's upturned faces in the
dark below the window. The basket wobbled on its rope as she started
to lower it. Half-way down, Uriah decided he'd had enough.

*It's only me, Uriah dear, I've come to save you.*

He started to turn round and
round inside, miaowing and
scratching at the lid. The basket
swung about wildly, banging against
the sitting-room window pane.

A light shone out. The window
was thrown open, and Captain
Grimthorpe put his head out,
peering into the darkness. At that
moment Uriah's nose appeared
under the lid of the basket.

In no time he had forced his way
out and, clinging on for a moment
with his claws, he made a great leap,
landing right on top of Captain
Grimthorpe's head!

There was a great uproar of wild
cries and oaths, and a flurry of
ginger curls. Uriah tore off into the
night, wearing a ginger wig –
and Captain
Grimthorpe
was quite bald!

Then a great many confusing things seemed to happen at once. They all crowded into the hall. Granny ran out of the kitchen, throwing her apron over her head and making a noise like a mad owl.

Bald Captain Grimthorpe stamped about, purple in the face with rage, calling for his wig. Mary was crying, "Oh, Uriah, come back, come back!" And the red-eyed dog barked fiercely at everybody.

At this moment little Arthur stepped bravely forward, and said in a calm, clear voice:

"Captain Grimthorpe doesn't look a bit like his portrait up there without his hair on. I don't believe he's the same man at all!"

There was a sudden silence. Granny came out from under her apron and peered into Captain Grimthorpe's face.

"My goodness, I do believe the lad's right. You're not the same gentleman as I remember – I can see that now, even without my glasses."

"His moustache doesn't look very real either," observed Jim, "it's sort of coming loose at one side."

Captain Grimthorpe's face flushed to scarlet, and so did his shiny bald head. Muttering something under his breath, he retreated upstairs with his red-eyed dog at his heels.

"I always thought there was something funny about him," said Mary. "But don't let's bother about him now, the horrid old thing. We've *got* to find Uriah."

For a long time they searched and called. It seemed hours before they heard an answering miaow, and Uriah came strolling up, shaking his back legs and pretending that nothing unusual had happened.

The next day Granny had some news for them. Captain Grimthorpe had disappeared! He had packed his things in the night and gone off with his dog, leaving nothing behind but a false moustache on the dressing-table.

Of course, he wasn't the real Captain Grimthorpe at all. It turned out that he was the Captain's lazy brother, Maurice, well known for his bad temper and dishonesty, who was going about in disguise to avoid paying his debts. Uriah had revealed his secret. Neither he nor his dog were ever seen again in those parts.

Soon afterwards some people from the Council called. As soon as Granny saw them, she let out a shriek and threw her apron over her head again. But they were politely trying to explain that Hardlock House was to be made into an Old Folk's Home, with the

Here's your tea, dear!

agreement of the *real* Captain Grimthorpe, and that Granny was to be one of the first to be offered a place there.

Hardlock House was soon transformed, with curtains in the windows, pretty papers on the walls and flowering plants everywhere.

Granny soon settled down happily to her new life, having her meals cooked for her, playing Bingo and watching the boxing on colour TV. She even got used to the other old folk, although she sometimes complained about them.

And Mary?

Jim and Arthur had grown so fond of her that she came to live at their house as one of the family, and they all three started school together when term began.

Uriah made himself at home, too, without being asked. The food was much better than what he had been used to at Hardlock House.

Of course, they all visited Granny often, and kept her up to date with their latest news.

As for the ginger wig, which Uriah had abandoned on a fence down by the railway footpath, it hung there forgotten all winter, blowing about in the wind.

But when the spring came a couple of sparrows made a nest in it, and settled down to raise a family.

# The Bird Child

A certain small girl once lived in a big city which had a forest on its northern edge and an orphanage on its southern edge. The little girl was an orphan herself. She had no father or mother, only an aunt. But this aunt was of the forgetful kind. One day, when they were having a picnic in the forest, the aunt forgot she had a little girl to look after. She wandered off home, packed her suitcase and went to South America. She was never heard of again.

The little girl waited and waited for her to come back. Fortunately the aunt had left her under a wild apple tree. She lay on her back watching the pattern of blue sky, green leaves and red apples. When the apples fell down she ate them. On the third day of waiting, two pigeons flew down and looked at the little girl very hard.

"Are you going to live here for ever?" they asked her, but the little girl was too small to explain that she had been left there by her aunt.

"My dear," said the father pigeon to the mother pigeon, "I think she has been left behind by some picnickers. They are always leaving eggshells and banana peel around. Now they have left a child."

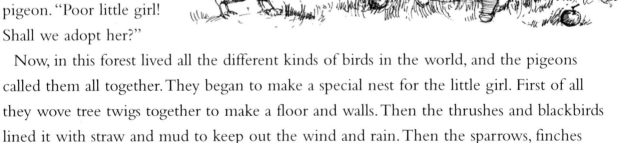

"It is very untidy of them," said the mother pigeon. "Poor little girl! Shall we adopt her?"

Now, in this forest lived all the different kinds of birds in the world, and the pigeons called them all together. They began to make a special nest for the little girl. First of all they wove tree twigs together to make a floor and walls. Then the thrushes and blackbirds lined it with straw and mud to keep out the wind and rain. Then the sparrows, finches and warblers lined it with moss and feathers for softness.

Working together, some of the strongest birds lifted the little girl into the nest. They brought her blackberries and grass seed to eat, and even a few worms. She just opened her mouth and they poked food into it.

It was much easier than living with the aunt who used to say, "Sit up straight and don't make a lot of crumbs when you eat."

As the weeks went by, the birds grew very fond of the little girl, and were always trying to think of ways to amuse her. Because she hated to see them fly away and leave her, they made her a pair of wings out of twigs and tree-gum and feathers. The little girl soon learned to use them cleverly. She flew with the birds in the sunshine. She soared and twisted in and out of the forest trees, chasing the birds and gathering her own blackberries and worms. Living like this she grew strong and brown and wild. Her hair was tangly, all full of leaves and flowers. Her clothes got torn to pieces and fell off, but this made it much simpler when she wanted to go swimming.

Every few months the birds made her a new pair of wings, brighter and stronger than those she had outgrown.

One day a hunter, hunting around, saw a flash of blue in the green trees. Flying on wings made by peacocks and kingfishers, the little girl spun into sight for a moment and then was lost again. The huntsman did not know that the birds had made her wings for her. He thought she had grown them all on her own. He went and brought back another hunter and a circus man. They set up a table in the middle of the forest with a birthday cake on it. Before long the Bird Child came down to look at it, and then the hunters threw nets over her. Her great wings broke and crumpled.

The hunters and the circus man were very angry when they found her wings were just tied on with ribbons woven of grass, but there was nothing they could do about it. So the hunters took the little girl out of the forest, right across the city to the orphanage. It was a square brown building in a square brown yard. The woman in charge was Mrs Parsley. She did not enjoy her job very much. She really wanted to spend her time growing tomatoes and strawberries. Instead, she had to look after thirty lively, grubby children. When the hunters gave her the Bird Child she was not pleased.

"Tisk! Tsk!" she went with her tongue and took the Bird Child inside. She scrubbed her and rubbed her but she could not make her pale like the other orphans. She could not brush her tangly hair either, so she snipped it off. She dressed the Bird Child

in a brown dress and put shoes on her feet, so that she could not run. The walls round the orphanage were tall as trees and there was a lock on the gate.

The little Bird Child grew thinner and quieter. She became paler than any of the other orphans. Mrs Parsley gave her cod-liver oil, but it did not make her better. (Mrs Parsley should have given her a beakful of honey or a few worms. But Mrs Parsley did not think of that.)

Once a week the Mayor of the city used to come and count the orphans. He was very proud of his neat, well-run orphanage.

"Where did the new orphan come from?" asked the Mayor. "She doesn't look to be a very good one."

"Some hunters found her in the forest," said Mrs Parsley. "You just don't know *where* orphans are going to turn up these days."

Just then the Mayor and Mrs Parsley heard a noise like the wind, though there was no wind. They looked up at the hills on the other side of the city and saw a cloud rise from the secret heart of the forest. It swirled and eddied like smoke, but it was not smoke. It shimmered and shivered like silk, but it was not silk. Mrs Parsley and the Mayor stared uneasily. The cloud came closer.

"It's birds," said Mrs Parsley, amazed.

"Birds!" cried the Mayor like an echo.

Sparrows, thrushes, blackbirds, peacocks, pigeons, parrots and pelicans, firebirds, pheasants and flamingos, swans and seagulls, egrets and eagles, herons, hummingbirds and various finches, all were flying straight towards the orphanage, making the air whisper and the leaves stir and rustle with the wind of their wings.

"Well, I've never seen so many birds!" said Mrs Parsley suspiciously. "It's not natural. They'll drop feathers all over the orphanage ground. And it's just been rolled and swept."

Down in the orphanage yard, one orphan looked up at the birds and cried out to them in a voice that was curious and lonely. She held up her arms as if she might fly up and join them. The cloud of birds wheeled and swept down, making a great storm. For a moment the Mayor and Mrs Parsley could see nothing but bright whirling feathers. Then the birds rose again and flew off towards the forest. They took all the orphans with them.

Mrs Parsley and the Mayor stared after them.

"Those birds have taken the Civic Orphans!" cried the Mayor. "And they haven't filled in any adoption forms."

The birds flew back to the forest. They had come to the orphanage looking for their Bird Child, but, because they could not tell one orphan from another, they had taken the lot. They carried all the orphans into the green shade of the forest, and began looking after them. First they built them nests, then they fed them with honey. The orphans sat in a row and the birds dropped honey into their open mouths. Then the birds made the orphans wings. All the orphans became Bird Children.

Mrs Parsley spent all that spring with a spade digging up the orphanage lawn. She grew the most remarkable tomatoes. On summer evenings she would look up from her garden to see the Bird Children, tossing like bright kites over the green roof of the forest, their wings wide and shining carrying them up towards the stars.

*written by Margaret Mahy*

# The Lion and the Unicorn

"London's burning,
London's burning!
Fetch the engines,
fetch the engines!
Fire, fire! Fire, fire!
Pour on water,
pour on water!"

Every evening, soon after dark, the warning sirens wailed. Then came the awful droning of enemy aircraft overhead, and fire-bombs and explosives whined and whistled out of the sky.

Lenny Levi and his mum huddled together under the stairs. Lenny clutched the badge that his dad had given him before he went away. It was made of solid brass; a lion and a unicorn up on their hind legs, fighting each other. Lenny kept it in his pocket always where he could feel it.

Dad was fighting too. He was in the army far away while Lenny and Mum clung to one another and longed for daylight.

A unicorn was a mythical beast, Dad had told him. A mysterious, gentle creature. But lions were real, all right.

Lions stood for being brave. Everybody had to be brave in wartime, not only soldiers but other people too. Children even. "Be a brave boy, Lenny," Dad had told him when they said goodbye.

Sometimes they got letters from Dad. They came in batches, two or three at a time. Those were the best days. Mum read bits out to Lenny while he was having his tea. Dad always put in a drawing for him. Sometimes it was a funny picture like the one of the Sergeant. Once he did a beautiful picture of a unicorn with flowers around its neck.

One night the bangs shook the house so badly that they thought the roof would fall in. "We should have gone to the shelter," muttered Mum.

Next morning, when they went out, the Robinsons' house wasn't there any more. Their things were lying all over the street amongst the rubble and broken glass. The neighbours said that the Robinsons had gone to the Rest Centre in the night, wearing blankets.

"That's it!" said Mum. "We've got to get you out of here, Lenny."

Soon, suitcase packed and his name on a label pinned to his jacket, clutching his precious badge in his pocket, Lenny joined a crowd of other children at the railway station. Mum was there to see him off.

Lenny felt the shape of the lion with his fingertips. He knew he was supposed to be brave. But when he saw so many strange faces he didn't know how to be.

"It'll be a lovely place in the country," Mum told him. "Flowers and rabbits and that." But she was nearly crying.

Lenny only realised what was really happening when he was in a crowded railway carriage. He put his head out of the window and shouted: "Don't leave me, Mum! You come with me!"

But the train had already started to move, very slowly at first, then fast gaining speed. "I'll come to see you soon!" called Mum. "Be a good boy." She was a white face amongst all the others. She shouted something else but Lenny couldn't hear her. Then she was a tiny figure at the end of the platform, waving and waving.

It was so dark when at last Lenny arrived that he could not see the place. The windows were blacked out. Then all at once he was in a huge hall, so big that it seemed their whole house in London could have fitted into it easily.

There were no rabbits that Lenny could see. Just some tired grownups bustling about, and two girls bigger than him who were called Joyce and Patsy, with a little one called Winnie. They were evacuees. Lenny was one too.

A lady wearing a great many scarves and woolly cardigans said: "I am Lady De Vass. You must be very tired. Nanny will give you your supper and show you where you are going to sleep."

'We specially asked for girls," Nanny complained, eyeing Lenny.

"I'm afraid it's too late now, Nanny," said Lady De Vass. "And he is not a very big boy," she added kindly.

The evacuees were to sleep in a big attic room with dark beams overhead. It was chilly and had no electric light or carpets but there was a nice woody smell.

A curtain hung down the middle.
Joyce, Patsy and Winnie were together
on one side and Lenny was alone on
the other.

Nanny left a couple of little lamps
burning when she said goodnight.
Lenny got down under the blankets.
He lay awake for a long time
watching the shadows moving in
the high roof. He could hear the
girls whispering behind the curtain,
then Winnie began to cry.

Lenny felt numb. The only thing
that seemed real at that moment was
the brass badge that Dad had given
him underneath his pillow. He went
to sleep clutching it.

Lenny woke very early while the
girls were still asleep. He could hear
faraway stirring noises in the house
and faint echoing footsteps, but no
one came. He got out of bed, pattered
over to the window and pulled the
blackout curtain aside.

His mouth fell open.

He looked out over a
jumble of roofs and
chimneys. Not the squat,
blackened kind like
they had in London

but a fairground of barley-sugar shapes with grinning gargoyle waterspouts winking in the sun. Beyond that, still wrapped in haze, were gardens, out-houses, meadows with great spreading trees and a humped-up hill rising behind like a cut-out paper shape.

So this was the country! He had never seen anything like it.

The great house which Lenny had come to was very old. It had countless rooms. Lady De Vass, who owned the place, lived in one part, Nanny in another. The army of servants who had once looked after the house and garden had now shrunk down to Mrs B. who cooked, Nelly who helped with the cleaning and washing up, and an old gardener called Bill Penny.

The evacuees had their breakfast in a kitchen as big as the synagogue Lenny went to at home. It was warm in there but Lenny was shy and miserable. Nelly smiled at him. There was porridge with plenty of milk and thick slices of bread and marge. But Mrs B. was cross when Lenny would not eat the bacon she gave him.

"There's good food wasted! I'll not have that!" she scolded. "We don't eat bacon in our family," said Lenny in a low voice.

Everyone stopped eating and stared at him. Joyce's eyes were as round and as hard as marbles. Even Winnie stopped grizzling. Lenny felt his ears turning pink. But he was stubborn. He thought of Mum and Dad and he still wouldn't eat the bacon. In the end Mrs B. gave in and told the children to take their dirty plates into the scullery and get out from under her feet.

The girls went off giggling, trailing Winnie after them. Lenny did not know what he was supposed to do so he wandered off into the yard, through a big gate and into the gardens.

He walked along paths with wide overgrown flowerbeds and peeped into long greenhouses. He found a goldfish pond like the one in the park at home but it was choked with weeds and the fish had gone.

There was a summerhouse half hidden in ivy and beyond it, set in a high stone wall, a wooden door.

It was not the door to somebody's house, Lenny knew that. It was a garden door. He remembered hearing somewhere about a secret garden that was locked up for years and years and nobody ever went in.

Cautiously he pushed the door. It creaked open.

Inside was a little garden, like a room without a roof. It had criss-cross mossy paths lined with knee-high hedges and stone seats. In the centre was a great rose bush with trailers which swept the ground.

It was very quiet in there. Then a bird flew up with a great clatter of wings and Lenny saw something on the far side of the garden, high up on a pedestal by the wall. At first he thought it was something alive and watching him. But it was too still to be alive. He went over to it.

It was a unicorn, carved in stone, just like the one on his badge. It did not look fierce. Strong, perhaps, and very beautiful, with its curved neck and long mane. Prancing there alone in the shadow of the wall it seemed as lonely as he was.

Lenny felt a huge relief to have found this place. It made him feel more like himself again. He made up his mind to come back there whenever he could.

On Monday morning the evacuees started at the village school. The children were not friendly. They looked at Lenny blankly as though he wasn't there. When the bell went for morning prayers Lenny had to stay alone in the classroom, sitting at a desk.

In the playground Joyce, Patsy and Winnie went off together. Lenny was not included in the boys' football game. He stood by the wall until it was time to go home, clutching Dad's badge in his pocket and pretending he didn't care.

On Saturday nights the evacuees had a bath and Nanny inspected their heads for nits. The bath was huge and had iron feet with claws like a lion. They were only allowed four inches of hot water (it was rationed, like almost everything else) and by the time it was Lenny's turn it wasn't even hot any more.

Joyce was Nanny's favourite. Nanny curled her hair for her and pressed her hair ribbons for church on Sunday. Joyce put on a special cute voice when she talked to grownups, but when the evacuees were on their own she was sharp-tongued and treacherous.

Lenny spent a lot of time wandering alone in the gardens where no one bothered him. One afternoon when he pushed open the door of the walled garden he found somebody else there. A young man with one leg was sitting on one of the stone benches. He was wearing an old tweed jacket with patched elbows. His empty trouser leg was pinned up and his crutches were propped neatly against the bench beside him.

"Hello there," said the man. "It's all right — I do live here. I was just trying to do a bit of weeding."

"Are you Bill Penny's helper?" Lenny asked him.

"Sort of," said the man. "I used to shoot

rabbits and pigeons when they
got into his vegetable garden but
I don't any more. This is one of my
favourite places."

Lenny hovered by the gate, not
sure what to say next.

"My name's Mick," the man
continued. "Don't let me having
one leg bother you."

"How did you lose it?" Lenny
wanted to know.

"I left it on a beach in France,"
the man told him. 'But I'll be
getting a new one soon."

"Will it be wooden?"

"No, light metal, I think. With
joints."

There was a friendly silence. Then
Lenny remembered he was not to
talk to strangers. He was not sure
whether as this man lived here he
counted as a stranger or not, but
he thought he had better be on
the safe side.

"I've got to go now," he said.

Mick just waved.

On wet days Lenny sometimes
followed Nelly about the house and
they chatted while she dusted and
polished.

In the great hall there was a suit of armour, swords hanging on the walls and pictures of battle scenes with soldiers in red coats. There was one full-length portrait of a very grand officer in splendid uniform.

"That's Lady De Vass's grandfather," said Nelly. "They've got a lot of soldiers in the family. Lady De Vass's husband was killed fighting in the First World War and her son's a war hero. He's got medals and all."

"My dad's in the army," Lenny told her.

"I'm joining up myself soon," said Nelly. "Women's Land Army."

Lenny longed for Mum to come but she wrote to say that she would not visit "until he had settled down". She was working in a fireman's canteen. She was not a good writer and her letters were short. But she saved up her sweet ration and sent Lenny a bar of chocolate now and again.

Lenny saw Mick about the place sometimes, helping Bill Penny or Lady De Vass, but he never came into the kitchen for his meals.

"There's something been killing rabbits in my vegetable garden," said Bill one afternoon when he was supping up his tea. "Not that I mind," he added, "I'm glad of it."

"A fox?" suggested Mrs B.

"No, it's never a fox. More like a big cat. It got some pigeons too."

"It'll be one of those wild cats that's living in the barn," said Mrs B. "Very fierce, they are."

"Or perhaps a lion escaped from the zoo," said Joyce slyly, looking sideways at Lenny. "Lions kill people. They wait in the dark and spring out at you and tear your stomach out."

That night, long after the others had gone to sleep, Lenny lay awake, listening to the night noises outside. Far away in the dark he thought he heard a growling, purring sound, then a shriek of an animal in pain. He got up and peeped through the curtains. Was there something prowling about? A black shadow moving alongside the hedge?

He hurried back into bed and pulled the blankets over his head.

Lenny thought about Mum and Dad a lot, hoping and hoping they were safe. He longed to see them again.

At school things had got a lot worse. The boys had started to shout things at him and make fun of his name.

"Lenny Levi's done a wee-wee!" they jeered. "Wets his bed, don't he?"

Lenny turned hot with anger and shame. It was true – about the bed. It was only sometimes, and he didn't think anyone at school knew about it. He guessed that Joyce must have told them.

Nanny was grim-faced in the mornings when she had to deal with wet sheets. But Nelly found out and came to Lenny's rescue.

"You can beat this, Lenny," she told him. "Everybody does in the end."

She smuggled some spare bedclothes into the attic so that Lenny could put them on before Nanny came in the morning.

She whisked away wet sheets and washed them herself. And she lent Lenny her big alarm clock. Lenny set it twice in the night and it went off with a great clang, but the girls never woke up.

The bedwetting got better. But the boys at school went on teasing.

One afternoon Mick came across Lenny sitting hunched on a bench in the walled garden and politely failed to notice his red-rimmed eyes.

"Homesick?" he asked.

At first Lenny was too upset to answer. Then he blurted out all about what the boys at school had said. "It's not even true any more! Well, hardly at all. But I don't suppose they'll ever stop saying it."

"I used to wet my bed when I was your age," Mick told him. "It was when they sent me away to boarding school."

"Had you done something wrong?" asked Lenny.

"No, they thought it would do me good," said Mick. "My father went there. It was awful. I got teased all the time. Then it started again when I was in hospital after..." He looked down at where his leg had been.

"But you were grown up then!" said Lenny, amazed.

"Yes. I cried a lot too. But I got through it somehow. And so will you, or my name's not Mick De Vass!"

There was a long silence. Lenny stared at Mick. "You're the war hero!" he said at last. "You've got medals for bravery – Nelly told me!"

"I was frightened all the time in the fighting," said Mick. "But I suppose you can't be brave if you're not frightened in the first place. My father was really brave, a fine officer. I am only a private."

"My dad's a private," said Lenny proudly. "He's fighting the Germans, like you did. I've got his badge."

"I never wanted to fight Germans or anyone else," Mick told him. "It's cruelty, bullying and oppression we're fighting against." Lenny was not quite sure what this meant but he got the general idea.

"I used to come here to this garden to see the unicorn when I was a boy in the school holidays," said Mick. "I used to long to be brave and manly and all the things they wanted me to be. But there are different kinds of courage. And I'll tell you one thing. The boys who say those things to you haven't got much. None at all, in fact!"

Later, when he was alone, Lenny thought a lot about what Mick had said. Gradually the bedwetting stopped altogether. Knowing a real war hero who had had the same problem helped. He even forgot about prowling lions.

But then something happened which was much worse.

Mum's weekly letters stopped coming. Every morning Lenny waited anxiously by the gates for the postman to arrive but there was nothing for him. He told nobody how worried he was. But he started to have bad dreams, about searching for Mum, and running and running, and lions leaping out at him and pinning him down with their terrible teeth and claws.

The bedwetting started again. In the end everything was just too terrible to be borne.

One night Lenny waited till the girls were asleep. He had his suitcase ready packed.

He put his precious badge in his pocket and crept downstairs to the back kitchen. It was difficult to unbolt the back door without making a noise but he managed it, standing on a chair.

He was running away. He had to get back to London.

He planned not to go by the main drive which went round the front of the house, in case he was seen. Instead he would cut through the gardens, into the orchard, through a hole in the hedge and across the field to the road.

There was a bright moon. Lenny's sharp shadow tracked him nimbly along the silent paths.

In the vegetable garden he scampered past raspberry beds and rows of staked-up runner beans where anyone, or anything, could be hiding.

When he reached the orchard he broke into a run, weaving from one tree trunk to another, crouching low over his suitcase. When he reached the hedge he stopped short.

He thought he heard something moving stealthily and carefully through the grass on the other side. He listened. The whole night seemed to be breathing, purring, growling. He was sure something was coming through the hole in the hedge.

Lenny did not stop to find out what it was. He dropped his suitcase and ran.

Now the dark, many-chimneyed shape of the house seemed to be flying swiftly against the moon, too far away to run to now. But he ran all the same, wildly, until he was heaving for breath. Now he was on the path by the summer-house. He saw the door to the walled garden. He pushed it open, fell inside and slammed it shut behind him.

Lenny was crying now, but he felt safe. The garden was completely quiet. The rosebush was frozen in the moonlight. Underneath, in its dense shadow, something glowed softly. It moved gently.

Lenny wasn't frightened. He went towards it. And at that moment he saw the unicorn.

It was alive, glimmering under the

rosebush, sitting on its haunches with its one spiralling horn and its long, white, silky mane. It turned its beautiful neck and looked at him.

Lenny knelt down. He laid his head between its hooves with his face in the grass. He was very tired. Almost at once he fell, as though from a great height, into a deep sleep.

He woke with the sun hot on his neck. It was morning and the unicorn had gone. The statue was in its usual place, watching over the garden.

Lenny got up and looked around. He knew that something had changed inside him. It seemed now that it was his own night fears which had been chasing him. He went out of the garden, closing the door softly behind him, and began to walk back to the house.

The lion and the unicorn were back inside Lenny's head; and on his badge. But one important thing was real, and that was what the unicorn stood for.

"Different kinds of courage," Mick had said. Now, after last night, Lenny thought he really knew what that meant. Perhaps with his new unicorn courage, he would try to stick things out for a bit and see if they got better. Anyway, he didn't seem to care much what Joyce and the rest of them said or did any more. They were only a load of mean, mangy old cats after all.

Lenny came to where the garden met the back drive. As he turned the bend he saw a figure coming towards the house from the opposite direction. A smallish person in a brown coat. A familiar walk. There was a good distance between them. Lenny quickened his pace. Then he broke into a run. Now, as he got closer, the outline of that person was blurred with tears.

Lenny tore the last few yards. "Mum – oh Mum!" he shouted. And he threw himself into her arms.

"Didn't you get my letter?" said Mum after a while.

"Bombed out. A direct hit – the whole house gone. Lucky I was working at the canteen that night."

"I never got no letter," sobbed Lenny. "The letterbox must have got it," said Mum. "I was running away," Lenny tried to tell her. "But then..." his voice choked. It was too difficult to explain.

"Lucky you didn't," said Mum, "or we might have missed each other. You're a brave boy, Lenny, a proper hero you are. After you left it seemed like even bombs would have been better than us being separated. But now I've come to take you away. We're going to your Auntie Rachel's in Wales. It's by the sea, Lenny. And guess what – your dad's coming home on leave! We'd better go and tell them."

Lenny felt in his pocket to check that his badge was safe. So he, Lenny Levi, was brave after all. He knew that didn't mean he would never be scared again. But at that moment, he felt he could face anything.

Jaunty now, and hand in hand with Mum, he walked towards the house.

# A cat may look at a king

*We all have a right to our own opinions, even about the most important people*

# Pride goes before a fall

*Self-important people come to grief sooner or later*

# It's no use crying for the moon

*There's no point hankering after something you know you can't have*

# It's no use crying over spilt milk

*Once you've made a mistake, worrying about it won't put things right*

# Here Comes Charlie Moon

*Charlie Moon and his cousin, Ariadne, are spending the summer holidays with their Auntie Jean who runs a joke shop at the seaside. At first there's not much to do except chase the thieving Morgan boys away from the shop, or visit Carlo Cornetto's Crazy Castle, with its shabby waxworks and dusty hall of mirrors. Then Auntie Jean meets Mrs Cadwallader, an old friend from her theatrical days, and things really start to liven up. Mrs Cadwallader organises an Old Time Night at the Crazy Castle, and the evening is a roaring success. But in the night, vandals break into the Castle and leave the place in a terrible mess. Charlie Moon is convinced that the Morgan boys are to blame, and he comes up with a secret plan to frighten them away for good.*

All the houses on Penwyn Bay front, from Auntie Jean's shop on the corner up to the Crazy Castle, have back yards giving on to a connecting alley-way, which is full of old cartons, broken milk-bottles and other dubious rubbish. It's a cat's kingdom, where Einstein haunts the dustbins at night, competing noisily with his enemies for tit-bits. But this evening, at dusk, all is quiet. Not a cat to be seen. The television sets are glowing blue-white against tightly drawn curtains, and only bursts of recorded studio laughter break the silence.

Auntie Jean, after evening Chapel, emerges from the front door of her shop and hurries away up the prom in the direction of the all-night launderette in Market Street, pushing the huge pramful of dirty washing which has been lying in wait for her all week. Soon after she has departed, Ariadne puts her head round the back gate which leads into the alley. Then she creeps out, leading the shuffling hairy figure of a gorilla. It is wearing a long mackintosh and floral headscarf. Almost immediately it trips on a squashed orange, falls down on its face, and has to be helped up and dusted off.

"I tell you, I can't see properly," says Charlie's voice crossly from somewhere inside the gorilla's mouth. "You're supposed to be leading me, aren't you?"

"All right. You'll get used to it soon. Hang on to me and try not to make such a row."

"It's too hot in here."

"Well!" says Ariadne, pulling him along. "That's typical! It was your great idea to dress up in that suit, left over from some pathetic panto at the old Royalty, and now you're grumbling about it already. I had enough trouble getting you into it."

"It's this scarf on top of the mask. It's suffocating me."

"You have to cover yourself up somehow until we get there, Charlie. Suppose we meet someone?"

"I didn't think this body part was going to be so uncomfortable. It must have been made for a dwarf."

"Hunch over a bit. It'll make you look more realistic."

It had seemed like a good idea to Charlie that afternoon to dress up in a gorilla suit, but now he's inside it he's not so sure. He'd had his eye on it ever since he arrived at Auntie Jean's and noticed it hanging behind the sitting-room door. The head part he found on a high shelf at the back of the shop. It has huge grinning teeth, flaring red nostrils, and deep eye-sockets under a shaggy fringe of hair. The body part is made of artificial fur, zips up the back, and is very dusty. Charlie thought he had managed to get rid of most of the dust by shaking the whole thing out of his bedroom window, but now he realises he hasn't been very successful. He seems to be hovering all the time on the edge of a sneeze. What's more, it smells nasty inside, and the eye-holes are too wide apart, so he can only see out by squinting down one nostril.

Of course Ariadne was all ready to be scathing when he explained his idea to her, how he meant to dress up and lie in wait at Mr Cornetto's place while he was out, in case whoever-it-was came back again.

"What do you want a *disguise* for?" she couldn't resist asking. "It'd be easy enough without the mask."

But she'd helped him into it and zipped him up the back all the same. She's even admitted that the effect was pretty good. They'd had to hide in the top bedroom until they'd seen Mrs Cadwallader and Mr Cornetto setting out, arm in arm in the summer dusk, for their walk on the pier. After that, it was an all too easy job to lure Lordy from his post as watch-dog with the help of a bowl of dog-meat. Ariadne has "borrowed" the spare key to Mr Cornetto's back door from its usual place on Auntie Jean's dresser. Lordy is, at this moment, very full and already dozing heavily in one of Auntie Jean's armchairs.

They creep along the alley-way and manage to reach the back door of the Crazy Castle without meeting a soul. Once again Ariadne puts the key into the lock, but she finds she has no need to turn it. She had forgotten to re-lock the door when she let Lordy out.

"Hey, wait a minute while I get these clothes off," says Charlie, struggling out of the headscarf and mackintosh. Together they fold and hide them behind Mr Cornetto's dustbin, then they creep inside the house.

At first it's too dark to see anything. They grope their way through the rear door of the Waxworks Hall. The rows of figures stand in uncanny stillness, muffled in their elaborate costumes. A faint light filters through a little cracked glass dome overhead, catching a sharp beak of a black profile here and there, a towering wig, a glittering glass eye. Ariadne finds her throat is dry, clears it, and is appalled by the loud noise it makes. It is much too quiet in here. Her superior attitude to the whole plan drains away suddenly. It seems impossible to speak in the presence of these listening shapes, and even more impossible to walk up the room between them. She flattens herself against the wall.

"Come on," says Charlie hoarsely, dragging her arm and shuffling forward. "You hide up here, behind the curtain over the archway. I'm going to be in the entrance hall."

"It isn't worth it, Charlie. Nobody's here. Nobody's going to come... are they?" Her voice trails off into a squeak of fright.

But Charlie is resolute. He pads off into the darkness. Unable to bear being left behind, Ariadne hurries after him, not daring to look on either side of her. She reaches the curtain and peers round it into the entrance hall beyond. She can make out only tables and chairs, neatly arranged after their labours that morning, ready for tomorrow. Charlie seems to have disappeared into thin air.

"Charlie?" she croaks into the blackness.

There is a muffled answer from the far corner. Charlie's gorilla shape is standing against the wall between the big wooden bear and a suit of armour, looking as much as possible like another waxwork figure.

"Hide behind the curtain," he hisses across the room. "We've got to lie in wait."

"But Charlie..."

"What?"

"Let's go home after all. I mean, nobody's going to turn up. It's all totally pathetically useless our being here."

Charlie doesn't answer.

"Mr Cornetto might come back and find us here, and we won't know how to explain."

A pause. Then:

"All right. Go, then. You go off home if you like. I'm staying."

"Don't be silly. I won't leave you on your own."

"Well, *hide.*"

Ariadne retreats behind her curtain and hides. Charlie stands stiffly in his corner, as much to attention as his gorilla suit allows. Darkness. Silence. Minutes heavily passing. Voices and footsteps are heard faintly from time to time on the prom outside, but they walk on by, and fade away. In what seems like an endless tunnel of time, nothing at all happens. Every now and then Charlie can be heard snuffling inside his gorilla mask.

But he is grimly determined not to give in - not for an hour at least. It was his idea, after all.

After a very long time, Ariadne is suddenly aware of a faint thud. It comes not from outside on the prom but somewhere inside the building. She listens, straining. Then there is another noise, a slight scuffling. Then a door opens slowly. It's the door behind her, right over the other side of the Waxworks Hall - the one she and Charlie came through themselves. Somebody is coming in the same way.

Ariadne presses her hand over her mouth to stop herself from calling out. Has Charlie heard too? Moving the curtain very slightly, and putting her eye to the narrow gap, she can see him still standing in his corner, absolutely still. Behind her she can see nothing at all, only hear the footsteps, creaking up the hall towards her. Now a black shape blots out her line of vision, then another. Two figures pass by, only inches away from her. She sees a shoulder, a bit of anorak, a glimpse of an ear, someone about her own height. They pass through into the entrance hall.

There is the sound of stumbling, of knocking into furniture. Then voices, suddenly loud. The Morgan boys, of course!

"Watch where you're stepping, boy. Want to get us nicked?"

"I can't see. Where's the counter?"

"Over here, where it was before, see? Come on."

"It's breaking and entering, Dai."

"Not if they leave the door open it isn't. That's asking us in. They ought to know better after the last time, only they're that daft."

"Where's the dog, then?"

"They haven't no dog."

"I've seen one hanging about here."

"Aaaach, come on. Let's get some grub. I fancy some crisps, anyway."

More clumsy stumbling against tables and chairs as they make their way across the hall in the dark. Then a sharp intake of breath. Slowly Charlie's arms have started to move.

"Whassat?"

"What?"

"Over there, in the corner. Something moved!"

Silence. Then:

"Getaway, it's only one of them stuffed waxwork things. We'll soon have that over."

"Not that one - the other! Hey, Dai, let's get out of here...DAI! It's *walking*! Aaaaaaaah!"

Slowly Charlie moves forward, all hunched up and hairy, with his arms up and his great mask-jaw poking forward out of its fringe of hair - which is the only way, in fact, he can see where he's going. He's a terrifying sight in the shadowy dark.

The two Morgan boys scramble and blunder against each other in their panic to get away from him. One knocks over a chair, nearly falls, staggers to his feet again, straight into the arms of the wooden bear which lurches forward on top of him. Letting out a yelping scream, he dodges away, so that it rocks and falls. Meanwhile Dai has bolted through the archway that leads to the other small lobby. His brother flees headlong after him. Charlie, arms clawing the air, follows relentlessly.

The Morgan boys now have no idea where they are. They crash about against the wall, knocking into slot-machines, trying to find the other door. Some glass is smashed. Suddenly a blood-curdling disembodied voice speaks right into their ears, repeating the same phrase over and over again:

"Only one person at a time, please...Only one person at a time, please..." Charlie stops short, momentarily off his guard. But then he recognises the voice of the "Speak-Your-Weight" machine. Jolted into action, it can't stop.

"Only one person at a time, please...Only one person at a time, please..."

The Morgan boys are now nearly demented with fear. Managing at last to wrench open the door that leads into the Hall of Mirrors, they hurl themselves through. Instantly they are confronted by an army of reflections, a forest of themselves, an endless moving mass of arms and legs.

"...one person at a time, please...Only one person at a time, please..." mocks the hollow voice behind them. But as they run through the maze of mirrors, more and more grotesque versions of their own faces gibber and leer at them. Suddenly they are brought up short against what seems like a dead end, a huge mirror cutting off their escape. Now, over the shoulders of their reflections, they see the monster that pursues them, with sunken eyes, hairy arms upraised, and awful fixed grin. There's a passage leading on to the left, but here more mirrors surround them, and now there seems to be not one monster but many, great gorilla shapes leaping up, with others crowding behind, all reaching out to grab them.

"Only one person at a time, please...Only one person at a time, please..." insists the voice in the darkness.

At last another door, and beyond it they see deliverance. The back door leading out into the yard. They see the evening sky, the ordinariness of the brick wall. With a great burst of speed, the Morgan boys are out of the door and over the wall in an instant, with Charlie still lumbering after them.

Ariadne, left behind her curtain, listens transfixed to the voice of the "Speak-Your-Weight" machine, going on and on until at last it starts to slow down.

"...person...at...time...please...only..."

Then, abruptly, it stops altogether.

Ariadne puts her head out and peers through the darkness of the entrance hall at the confusion left behind by the rout of the Morgan boys.

"Charlie?" she calls quietly.

No reply.

She takes a few steps out from her hiding-place and calls again. Still no answer. Charlie has gone.

She hesitates fearfully, trying to remember where the light-switch is. She starts to feel her way along the wall, searching desperately. No switch. She finds herself blundering back through the curtains of the archway into the Hall of Waxworks again. Here, at least, there is a little light. But now she is alone with those stiffly posed figures, they appear even more terrifying - Dick Turpin with his pistols raised, the Executioner with his evil axe. To get to the back door she must somehow walk the length of the room, exposed to all those glassy eyes. She measures the distance, trying to pluck up courage. She knows that, besides the set-piece of Mary Queen of Scots, there are eight waxworks on each side of the aisle. Head down, eyes on the ground, she starts off. If you look at the feet, not the faces, it isn't so frightening. What's frightening about eight pairs of feet? She counts out of the corner of her eye. One, two, three, four, five...nearly there...six, seven...quick! quick!... eight, nine...

Suddenly she stops dead, her hand actually on the door handle.

Nine?

That's one pair extra.

Slowly, slowly she turns, eyes still down, and counts again. Six, seven, eight... She raises her eyes. Far down at the end of the hall, the end she's just come from, there is a faint rustle. The ninth waxwork is moving.

Ariadne shapes her mouth to a wild scream of fright, but no sound comes out. Flinging open the door, she bolts into the gathering dusk.

# Angel on the Roof

One bright moonlit night an angel landed on the roof of Number 32 Paradise Street, just east of Ladbroke Grove. He was attracted by the address. He had temporarily lost contact with base and needed to alight to give his wings a rest. He had flown over, but avoided, All Saints Road. Saints were in a different section where he came from.

Nobody noticed he was up there. Mr Gantry, who lived alone on the top floor, heard some scratching noises overhead but he put it down to pigeons. The Sharples family, still awake (they kept all hours), were too busy playing their radio very loud and shouting at each other to pay any attention. And Miss Babs Ridezski, who lived beneath them on the ground floor, was out at work, toiling long hours into the night in a big hotel. Even if she had been at home she would have heard nothing. She had accustomed herself to sleep through anything. Lewis Brown, who lived with his Mum and Dad in the basement flat, was too far down to notice.

The angel had come a long way and he was tired. He folded himself in his wings and slept. When he woke it was early, far too early for anyone in Paradise Street to be up and about. Nobody saw him hop up onto the chimney stack, spread his wings wide and give them a good shake. He beat them briskly to and fro. A golden feather fell out and spiralled gently downwards. Lewis Brown was the only person in the house who was awake. He was looking out of his barred bedroom window waiting for the day to begin. There wasn't much of a view. A brick wall, a glimpse of the street through the railings. He was looking forward to later in the morning when there would be legs hurrying past, fat legs, shapely legs, stumpy legs and long legs; legs wearing expensive shoes and legs with roller skates attached. Lewis thought a good deal about legs. One of his own legs was not quite like other people's. It was thinner than his good one and not so strong. It bowed out a bit. It made him slow getting up the basement area steps. So he didn't go out much. He preferred to sit by his window watching the legs go by rather than hang about in the street where he thought the other boys were staring at him. Girls too, giggling.

So it was Lewis who spotted the golden feather as it fluttered down and landed on his windowsill. He unlocked the basement door and went outside to pick it up. It felt warm in his hand. He knew it wasn't a pigeon's feather or one from Mr Gantry's canary. They were pearly grey or bright yellow and this one was pure shimmering gold, tinged with pink.

Lewis tipped back his head and squinted up at the roof. The sun was coming up behind the chimneys. It caught something brilliant and alive which trapped the sun's rays and held them, pulsing so brightly that it made him blink. He fetched the key to the main door of the house, slipped through the dim hall and climbed the stairs. He had to stop and rest his bad leg on every landing. At last he reached the door which led to the roof, unbolted it and stepped out into the sunny morning. The angel,

who was sitting with his back to a chimney stack, stood up. His outline was slightly blurred, a little tentative like a quick sketch. Solid too. His head shimmered and whirred faintly like a spinning top. But the radiant smile was unmistakable.

And that was the beginning of their great friendship.

It was Lewis, usually such a quiet self-contained boy, who did all the talking. He spent hours that day, and the days that followed, talking to the angel. The angel himself did not have the power of human speech but showed with his head and hands that he completely understood. They sat on the roof that first day as the sun edged overhead from morning into evening, while Lewis fearlessly told him things he had never mentioned to anyone before. About his ambition to be an athlete, and how he wished he could make friends more easily, and how miserable he felt when Dan Sharples turned up the volume of his Walkman when they met on the stairs and pretended he didn't hear when Lewis said 'Hello'. And, worst of all, the boiling irritation he felt with his mother, who he loved, when she wore her anxious expression to ask him how he had been getting on at school and urged him to get out more and play with the other boys. The angel took all this in, and much more, with his beautiful ears as transparent as glass, and Lewis felt a lot better for the telling.

Lewis offered to bring the angel something to eat and drink but he did not seem to need human nourishment. He liked just sitting and looking.

He would keep quite still and gaze at the sky for hours at a time. Lewis sat with him and gazed too. Oh, that sky! Lewis felt he was seeing it for the first time above the clogged city haze, the trailing shapes of clouds and infinite variety of colour.

Lewis fetched a baggy old overcoat belonging to his dad and the angel put it on to cover his wings. Together they descended from the rooftop and walked about in the streets. The angel hardly seemed to notice the shop windows. But he liked to look up at the complicated outlines of dormers, attics and crumbling cornices above, the skeletal arms of television aerials pointing heavenwards. He savoured the intricate patterns of old bicycles and washing hanging out and glimpses of people's lives through high windows. And he loved it when it rained.

"Your friend got a bad back, has he?" asked the boys who loitered outside the house. "Lewis Brown's going around with a hunchback now," they sniggered to one another. "Funny looking guy, isn't he?" But Lewis's Mum was delighted that he had found a friend. She knew from his face that he was happier and more complete in himself than he had been since a child.

Things at Number 32 began to change very slightly. Nothing much to notice, only what might be expected with an angel on the roof. Mr Gantry, for instance, seemed more cheerful. At least he did not grumble so much. Mr and Mrs Sharples went on shouting at each other but their voices lost the jarring edge of anger. They even turned their radio

down when Miss Ridezski was asleep. Lewis's Mum and Dad took to occasionally fetching the canary food for Mr Gantry from the market. One evening they even asked him down to watch television with them. And, most surprisingly, Lewis met Dan Sharples on the stairs without his Walkman (he only wore it all the time to block out the sound of his parents quarrelling) and they had a bit of a chat.

It was the school holidays. Nobody bothered to wonder why Lewis spent so much time up on the roof or wandering the streets with his new friend. Together they strolled through the debris of the stalls when the market was closing down, and in the quiet evenings among the discreetly wealthy houses on the higher slopes of Notting Hill, looking in at the bosky gardens behind the iron railings.

And all the time one idea was growing in Lewis's mind. He thought and thought about it until at last he could not keep it to himself a single minute longer. He climbed the stairs and found the angel sitting as usual with wings folded.

"You are my friend, aren't you?" Lewis blurted out. "You're my best friend – the best I ever had – you are, aren't you?"

The angel held out his hand.

"You're an angel – you've got wings. You can do miracles if you want, can't you? I mean, like a real magician?" Lewis knelt down and put his face very near to the angel's and said in a low voice: "Will you work a miracle for me? Will you make my leg better? Can you make it as strong as my good one? Will you do that for me?"

The angel simply sat in silence holding onto Lewis's hand.

"Please will you do it - please?" whispered Lewis. The angel just looked at him. And it seemed to Lewis that he had become slightly transparent. Not only his ears but his whole form appeared faded, insubstantial.

After a while Lewis let go of his hand and stood up, dully.

"You can't do it, can you?" he said. "You can't do proper miracles. Or else you won't!" Then he flung away and walked to the top of the stairs. When he looked back the angel was still in the same place, motionless by the chimney stack.

That night Lewis was too miserable to sleep. He lay awake staring at the moonlight on his bedroom ceiling. Then he heard a tapping at the window. The angel was outside, strong and solid as before but now he gave off a silver glow like the moon. When Lewis joined him he knew that something astonishing was going to happen. The angel took him in his arms, spread his wings and up they flew together out of the basement and into the warm night.

This must be a dream, thought Lewis.

Together they swung out over the city towards the river Thames, soaring over elegant cast iron bridges, Gothic parliamentary pinnacles, huge office blocks with glowing insomniac computer screens, over a great winking tower, a mighty river barrier, to mudflats and the ever widening estuary until they came to the sea. Then the angel swooped down until he was flying low over the waves and dropped Lewis in.

He hit the water with a great splash and came up spluttering. He had never tried to swim before because of his bad leg, but he wasn't in the least afraid. It was easy. He cast off his clothes and struck out strongly, carried upwards on the swell, heading into the breakers, lying on his back and kicking up spray. And the angel flew just above him, dipping and hovering like a great seabird.

It was a wonderful night, the best of Lewis's life. He was so happy and tired that he hardly noticed when at last the angel lifted him up, flew with him back to Paradise Street and set him down, still dripping, on the roof. They stood together side by side and watched the sun come up. When the first rays struck them Lewis noticed that there was only one shadow on the roof. The angel's body seemed to be melting into the sunshine.

"Don't leave me!" he cried in alarm.

The angel merely smiled and took both his hands for a moment. Then he spread his wings and flew onto the chimney stack where he stood, poised. All at once Lewis knew that nothing on earth would stop him from going.

"Goodbye!" he called bravely.

Now the angel's wings were beating fast. He was brim full of light.

"Goodbye, and thank you..." Lewis shouted, "thank you for..." His words trailed lamely away as he saw his friend rise up in the air, hover for a moment, then circle wide over Paradise Street. "Thank you for everything..." Lewis called after him. He felt the rush of wings, glimpsed a pair of heels shooting heavenwards, and then the angel was gone. Lewis blinked his eyes, which were full of tears. He noticed his Dad's old overcoat left lying neatly folded on the tiles. He put it on and walked slowly downstairs.

After that things went on much the same in Paradise Street. Well, not quite the same. Lewis knew, although of course he told nobody, that some traces of the angel were left behind. A less shrill feeling, some small kindnesses, an occasional unexplained waft of flowers on the stairs. And once, in the quiet mid-afternoon, they heard Miss Ridezski singing in a high, clear yearning voice in a language they could not understand. Then even the Sharples family switched their radio off to listen.

Importantly, Lewis found that he had not forgotten how to swim. He and his new friend Dan Sharples went to the swimming pool together two or three times a week, and when he was in the water Lewis forgot his bad leg altogether and felt just the same as everyone else.

Best of all, he had not forgotten how to look. Which is how he started to become a painter. And years later, when he was grown up, people took great pleasure in having their own eyes opened by his pictures; the skies and chimney pots, ebullient rooftops, sharp bird's-eye perspectives, the deeply etched shapes of old bicycles and airy flights of hung out washing.

"That Lewis Brown paints like an angel," they said.

# List of Shirley Hughes' Books for Children

Author and Illustrator:

Lucy and Tom's Day, Gollancz, 1960; The Trouble with Jack, The Bodley Head, 1970; Lucy and Tom Go to School, Gollancz, 1973; Sally's Secret, The Bodley Head, 1973; Helpers, The Bodley Head, 1975; Lucy and Tom at the Seaside, Gollancz, 1976; Dogger, The Bodley Head, 1977; It's Too Frightening For Me!, Hodder and Stoughton, 1977; Moving Molly, The Bodley Head, 1978; Up and Up, The Bodley Head, 1979; Here Comes Charlie Moon, The Bodley Head, 1980; Lucy and Tom's Christmas, Gollancz, 1981; Alfie Gets in First, The Bodley Head, 1981; Alfie's Feet, The Bodley Head, 1982; Charlie Moon and the Big Bonanza Bust-up, The Bodley Head, 1982; Alfie Gives a Hand, The Bodley Head, 1983; An Evening at Alfie's, The Bodley Head, 1984; Lucy and Tom's ABC, Gollancz, 1984; Chips and Jessie, The Bodley Head, 1985; Bathwater's Hot, Walker Books, 1985; When We Went to the Park, Walker Books, 1985; Noisy, Walker Books, 1985; Another Helping of Chips, The Bodley Head, 1986; Colours, Walker Books, 1986; All Shapes and Sizes, Walker Books, 1986; Lucy and Tom's 123, Gollancz, 1987; The Big Alfie and Annie Rose Storybook, The Bodley Head, 1988; Out and About, Walker Books, 1988; Angel Mae, Walker Books, 1989; The Big Alfie Out of Doors Storybook, The Bodley Head, 1992; The Snow Lady, Walker Books, 1992; Stories by Firelight, The Bodley Head, 1993; Giving, Walker Books 1993; Bouncing, Walker Books, 1993; Shirley Hughes Baby Record Book, Hutchinson, 1993; The Alfie Treasury, The Bodley Head, 1994; Chatting, Walker Books, 1994; Hiding, Walker Books, 1994; The Nursery Collection, Walker Books, 1994; Rhymes for Annie Rose, The Bodley Head, 1995; All Shapes and Sizes, Walker Books, 1995; Enchantment in the Garden, The Bodley Head, 1996; Tales of Trotter Street, Walker Books, 1996; Alfie and the Birthday Surprise, The Bodley Head, 1997; Alfie's Alphabet, The Bodley Head, 1997; Being Together, Walker Books, 1997; Playing, Walker Books, 1997; The Nursery Collection, Walker Books, 1997; The Lion and the Unicorn, The Bodley Head, 1998; The Charlie Moon Collection, Red Fox, 1998; Let's Join In, Walker Books, 1998; Wheels, Walker Books, 1999; Lucy and Tom's 123 and ABC, Hamish Hamilton, 1999; Alfie's Numbers, The Bodley Head, 1999; Abel's Moon, The Bodley Head, 1999; Helping, Walker Books, 1999; Big Concrete Lorry, Walker Books 1999; Wheels, Walker Books, 1999.

As Illustrator:

The Hill War by Olivia Fitzroy, 1950; Great Uncle Toby by John Hale, 1951; Mrs Dale's Bedside Book, 1951; World's End Was Home by Nan Chauncy, 1952; Follow the Footprints by William Mayne, 1953; The World Upside Down by William Mayne, 1954; The Journey of Johnny Rew by Anne Mainwaring Barrett, 1954; All Through the Night by Rachel Field, 1954; The Bell Family by Noel Streatfeild, 1954; Mr Punch's Cap by Kathleen Fidler, 1956; The Man of the House by Allan Campbell McLean, 1956; William and the Lorry by Diana Ross, 1956; Guns in the Wild by Ian Serraillier, 1956; Lost Lorrenden by Mabel Esther Allan, 1956; Katy at Home by Ian Serraillier, 1957; Adventure on Rainbow Island by Dorothy Clewes, 1957; The Jade Green Cadillac by Dorothy Clewes, 1958; The Boy and the Donkey by Diana Pullein-Thompson, 1958; Katy at School by Ian Serraillier, 1959; The Lost Tower Treasure by Dorothy Clewes, 1960; New Town by Noel Streatfeild, 1960; Rolling On by Mary Cockett, 1960; Flowering Spring by Elfrida Vipont, 1960; Fell Farm Campers by Marjorie Lloyd, 1960; The Bronze Chrysanthemum by Sheena Porter, 1960; The Painted Garden by Noel Streatfeild, 1961; The Singing Strings by Dorothy Clewes, 1961; Mary Ann Goes to Hospital by Mary Cockett, 1961; Fairy Tales by Hans Christian Andersen, 1961; Plain Jane by Barbara Softly, 1961; The Railway Children, by E Nesbit, 1961; Cottage by the Lock by Mary Cockett, 1962; Place Mill by Barbara Softly, 1962; The Merry-Go-Round by Diana Ross, 1963; Willy Is My Brother by Peggy Parish, 1963; Tales of Tigg's Farm by Helen Morgan, 1963; Meet Mary Kate by Helen Morgan, 1963; The Shinty Boys by Margaret MacPherson, 1963; Fiona on the Fourteenth Floor by Mabel Esther Allan, 1964; Operation Struggle by Dorothy Clewes, 1964; A Stone in a Pool by Barbara Softly, 1964; Tim Rabbit's Dozen by Alison Uttley, 1964; Roller Skates by Ruth Sawyer, 1964; The Cat and Mrs Cary by Doris Gates, 1964; Stories from Grimm by Roger Lancelyn Green, 1964; Stories for Seven-Year-Olds [Six-Year-Olds, Five-Year-Olds, Under-Fives, Nine-Year-Olds] and More Stories for Seven-Year-Olds, all edited by Sara and Stephen Corrin, 6 vols, 1964-79; A Dream of Dragons by Helen Morgan, 1965; Lucinda's Year of Jubilo by Ruth Sawyer, 1965; The Twelve Dancing Princesses by Margaret Storey, 1965;

Kate and the Family Tree by Margaret Storey, 1965; Tales the Muses Told by Roger Lancelyn Green, 1965; Satchkin Patchkin by Helen Morgan, 1966; The Smallest Doll by Margaret Storey, 1966; The Smallest Bridesmaid by Margaret Storey, 1966; The Faber Book of Nursery Stories edited by Barbara Ireson, 1966; The Witch's Daughter by Nina Bawden, 1966; Little Bear's Pony by Donald Bisset, 1966; Wayland's Keep by Angela Bull, 1966; Porterhouse Major by Margaret J Baker, 1967; Home and Away by Ann Thwaite, 1967; Mary Kate and the Jumble Bear [School Bus,] 2 vols, by Helen Morgan, 1967-70; The Toffee Join by William Mayne, 1968; The Sign of the Unicorn by Mabel Esther Allan, 1968; The New Tenants by Margaret MacPherson, 1968; A Day on Big O by Helen Cresswell, 1968; A Crown for a Queen by Ursula Moray Williams, 1968; The Toymaker's Daughter by Ursula Moray Williams, 1968; Flutes and Cymbals edited by Leonard Clark, 1968; Mrs Pinny and the Blowing Day [Sudden Snow, Salty Sea Day], 3 vols, by Helen Morgan, 1968-72; My Naughty Little Sister series by Dorothy Edwards, 9 vols, 1968-82; The Bicycle Wheel by Ruth Ainsworth, 1969; Moshie Cat by Helen Griffiths, 1969; The Wood Street Group by Mabel Esther Allan, 1970; The Wood Street Secret by Mabel Esther Allan, 1970; More Fairy Tales by Hans Christian Andersen, 1970; Rainbow Pavement by Helen Cresswell, 1970; Malkin's Mountain revised edition by Ursula Moray Williams, 1970; The Three Toymaker's revised edition by Ursula Moray Williams, 1970; The Ruth Ainsworth Book by Ruth Ainsworth, 1970; Cinderella by Charles Perrault, 1970; Eight Days to Christmas by Geraldine Kaye, 1970; The Wood Street Rivals by Mabel Esther Allan, 1971; Mother Farthing's Luck by Helen Morgan, 1971; Squib by Nina Bawden 1971; Frederico by Helen Griffiths, 1971; The Lost Angel by Elizabeth Goudge, 1971; The Smell of Privet by Barbara Sleigh, 1971; Burnish Me Bright by Julia W Cunningham, 1971; The Little Broomstick by Mary Stewart, 1971; Dancing Day by Robina Willson, 1971; Ginger by Geraldine Kaye, 1972; The Thirteen Days of Christmas by Jenny Overton, 1972; A House in the Square by Joan G Robinson, 1972; Hospital Day by Leila Berg, 1972; Mother's Help by Susan Dickinson, 1972; The First [Second, Third] Margaret Mahy Story Book, 3 vols, 1972-75; The Wood Street Helpers by Mabel Esther Allan, 1973; The Hollywell Family by Margaret Kornitzer, 1973; The Phantom Fisherboy by Ruth Ainsworth, 1974; The Gauntlet Fair by Alison Farthing, 1974; Jacko and Other Stories by Jean Sutcliffe, 1974; Miss Hendy's House by Joan Drake, 1974; Hazy Mountain by Donald Bisset, 1975; Away from Wood Street by Mabel Esther Allan, 1976; Peter Pan and Wendy retold by May Byron, 1976; The Snake Crook by Ruth Tomalin, 1976; Donkey Days by Helen Cresswell, 1977; The Phantom Roundabout by Ruth Ainsworth, 1977; Make Hay While the Sun Shines edited by Alison Abel, 1977; A Throne for Sesame by Helen Young, 1977; Stories for Eight-year-olds and Other Young Readers by Sara Corrin and Stephen Corrin (ed), 1977; From Spring to Spring by Alison Uttley, 1978; Bog Woppit by Ursula Moray Williams, 1978; Trouble with Dragons by Oliver Selfridge, 1978; The Snailman by Brenda Sivers, 1978; Pottle Pig by Nancy Northcote, 1978; The Pirate Ship and Other Stories by Ruth Ainsworth, 1980; Witchdust by Mary Welfare, 1980; Over the Moon, A Book of Sayings edited by Shirley Hughes, 1980; A Cat's Tale by Rikki Cate, 1982; Five to Eight by Dorothy Butler, 1985; Mahy Magic by Margaret Mahy, 1986; The Secret Garden by Frances Hodgson Burnett, 1988; My Naughty Little Sister and Bad Harry by Dorothy Edwards, 1990; My Naughty Little Sister's Friend by Dorothy Edwards, 1990; Little Women by Louisa M Alcott, 1994; Babies Need Books by Dorothy Butler, Penguin Books, 1995; The Complete 'My Naughty Little Sister' by Dorothy Edwards, 1997; Tell Me About Writers and Illustrators, by Chris Powling, 1999.

As Editor:

Collins Mother and Child Treasury, illustrated by Clara Vulliamy, HarperCollins, 1998.

# ACKNOWLEDGEMENTS

'Fingers' from RHYMES FOR ANNIE ROSE © 1995 Shirley Hughes. Published by The Bodley Head.

'Toes' from RHYMES FOR ANNIE ROSE © 1995 Shirley Hughes. Published by The Bodley Head.

'Bathwater's Hot' © 1985 Shirley Hughes from THE SHIRLEY HUGHES NURSERY COLLECTION. Reproduced by permission of the publisher, Walker Books Ltd., London. With thanks to the publisher.

'Bernard' from RHYMES FOR ANNIE ROSE © 1995 Shirley Hughes. Published by The Bodley Head.

'Girl Friends' from RHYMES FOR ANNIE ROSE © 1995 Shirley Hughes. Published by The Bodley Head.

'Mudlarks' © 1988 Shirley Hughes from OUT AND ABOUT. Reproduced by permission of the publisher, Walker Books Ltd., London. With thanks to the publisher.

'Wind' © 1988 Shirley Hughes from OUT AND ABOUT. Reproduced by permission of the publisher, Walker Books Ltd., London. With thanks to the publisher.

LUCY AND TOM AT THE SEASIDE © 1976 Shirley Hughes. Reproduced by permission of the publisher, Puffin Children's Books. With thanks to the publisher.

'A Picture of Annie Rose' from RHYMES FOR ANNIE ROSE © 1995 Shirley Hughes. Published by The Bodley Head.

'Wet' © 1988 Shirley Hughes from OUT AND ABOUT. Reproduced by permission of the publisher, Walker Books Ltd., London. With thanks to the publisher.

'Misty' © 1988 Shirley Hughes from OUT AND ABOUT. Reproduced by permission of the publisher, Walker Books Ltd., London. With thanks to the publisher.

'Cold' © 1988 Shirley Hughes from OUT AND ABOUT. Reproduced by permission of the publisher, Walker Books Ltd., London. With thanks to the publisher.

DOGGER © 1977 Shirley Hughes. Published by The Bodley Head.

UP AND UP © Shirley Hughes 1979. Published by The Bodley Head.

'Creepy Crawly World' from THE BIG ALFIE OUT OF DOORS STORY-BOOK © 1992 Shirley Hughes. Published by The Bodley Head.

'Fallen Giant' from THE BIG ALFIE OUT OF DOORS STORYBOOK © 1992 Shirley Hughes. Published by The Bodley Head.

ALFIE GIVES A HAND © 1983 Shirley Hughes. Published by The Bodley Head.

'Birthday' from THE BIG ALFIE AND ANNIE ROSE STORYBOOK © 1988 Shirley Hughes. Published by The Bodley Head.

'Bonting' from THE BIG ALFIE OUT OF DOORS STORYBOOK © 1992 Shirley Hughes. Published by The Bodley Head.

'Sea Sound' from THE BIG ALFIE OUT OF DOORS STORYBOOK © 1992 Shirley Hughes. Published by The Bodley Head.

'Here Comes the Bridesmaid' from THE BIG ALFIE AND ANNIE ROSE STORYBOOK © 1988 Shirley Hughes. Published by The Bodley Head.

'People in the Street' from THE BIG ALIFE AND ANNIE ROSE STORYBOOK © 1988 Shirley Hughes. Published by The Bodley Head.

'My Naughty Little Sister at the Party' text © 1952 Dorothy Edwards, illustrations © 1969 Shirley Hughes. Reproduced by permission of the publisher, Egmont Children's Books Ltd. With thanks to the publisher.

'Statue' from THE BIG ALFIE AND ANNIE ROSE STORYBOOK © 1988 Shirley Hughes. Published by The Bodley Head.

ABEL'S MOON © 1999 Shirley Hughes. Published by The Bodley Head.

'Moon' from THE BIG ALFIE OUT OF DOORS STORYBOOK © 1992 Shirley Hughes. Published by The Bodley Head.

'Wild Weather' from STORIES BY FIRELIGHT © 1993 Shirley Hughes. Published by The Bodley Head.

CINDERELLA text © 1970 Kathleen Lines, illustrations © 1970 Shirley Hughes. Published by The Bodley Head.

ANGEL MAE © 1989 Shirley Hughes. Reproduced by permission of the publisher, Walker Books Ltd., London. With thanks to the publisher.

'Coming Soon' from STORIES BY FIRELIGHT © 1993 Shirley Hughes. Published by The Bodley Head.

'Sea Singing' from STORIES BY FIRELIGHT © 1993 Shirley Hughes. Published by The Bodley Head.

'The By-Gone Fox' from CHIPS AND JESSIE © 1985 Shirley Hughes. Published by The Bodley Head.

ENCHANTMENT IN THE GARDEN © 1996 Shirley Hughes. Published by The Bodley Head.

IT'S TOO FRIGHTENING FOR ME © 1977 Shirley Hughes. Reproduced by permission of the publisher, Puffin Children's Books. With thanks to the publisher.

'The Bird Child' from THE SECOND MARGARET MAHY STORY-BOOK text © 1973 Margaret Mahy, illustrations © 1973 J. M. Dent. Reproduced by permission of the publisher, Orion Children's Books. With thanks to the publisher.

THE LION AND THE UNICORN © 1998 Shirley Hughes. Published by The Bodley Head.

'Pride Goes Before a Fall' from MAKE HAY WHILE THE SUN SHINES illustrations © 1977 Shirley Hughes. Reproduced by permission of the publisher, Faber and Faber Limited. With thanks to the publisher.

'A Cat May Look at a King' from MAKE HAY WHILE THE SUN SHINES illustrations © 1977 Shirley Hughes. Reproduced by permission of the publisher, Faber and Faber Limited. With thanks to the publisher.

'It's No Use Crying Over Spilt Milk' from MAKE HAY WHILE THE SUN SHINES illustrations © 1977 Shirley Hughes. Reproduced by permission of the publisher, Faber and Faber Limited. With thanks to the publisher.

HERE COMES CHARLIE MOON © 1980 Shirley Hughes. Published by The Bodley Head.

ANGEL ON THE ROOF © 2000 Shirley Hughes. First published in this edition by The Bodley Head.